ROUGH CHOICE

SCREAMING DEMONS MC
BOOK THREE

SUMMER COOPER
SIENNA CHANCE

LOVY BOOKS

1

The door crashed open so harshly, the knob left a large crack in the wall. Kye stormed inside and immediately flew into the kitchen where he grabbed two fistfuls of Grier's shirt and slammed him into the fridge that rattled loudly.

"Where is she?" Kye roared as though possessed. Grier, whose feet were dangling nearly six inches off the floor, pushed Kye, but the man was unwavering. Slamming him against the fridge again, Kye resisted punching him in the face.

"Relax!" Grier snapped as he struggled to free himself. "She's in the living room." Kye dropped him so hard that Grier stumbled forward and into the counter. Kye was already moving across the house until he entered the darkened living room.

"Eli!" he called and fumbled on the wall to turn on

the light. When he did, he saw her sitting motionlessly on the couch with a shoebox next to her. "Oh my God," he said, racing to her. Sliding on his knees in front of her, he took her face in his hands. Her face was covered in purple bruises. When he lightly touched one and she didn't flinch in the slightest, his brow furrowed.

"They're fake," Grier said from the doorway. Kye glanced up from Eliana for the briefest moment to look at the blonde. "We had to make it look convincing," Grier elaborated. Looking back down at Eliana, he noticed she was trembling slightly. Her bottom lip was swollen.

"This doesn't look fake," Kye said through gritted teeth as he glared up at Grier.

"She did that herself," Grier said, waving a hand through the air.

"I bit it," Eliana said quietly. "I was scared… scared to die."

"You're not going to die. I told you— I'm going to keep you safe," Kye said hurriedly. Eliana was already shaking her head.

"No," she said, meeting his gaze with her watery eyes. "The gun… I shot… the gun Grier gave me, I pulled the trigger. To shoot myself."

"You shot yourself?" he shouted and began looking her over, frantically searching for a bullet wound.

"Not exactly," Grier added as he leaned against the doorframe.

"Someone had better start explaining really fucking fast," Kye raged as he stood to his feet. "I saw that photo. Eliana looked dead. These bruises look pretty fucking real, and now you're saying she didn't 'exactly' shoot herself?"

"Grier said it was a test," Eliana began. Her voice was trembling more severely than her body. "Max was going to kill you if you didn't agree to his terms. We knew that. Grier had a plan, to send proof to Max that I was already dead so you didn't have to decide. He was either going to help me fake my death, or he was going to kill me."

"You were going to kill her?" Kye asked vehemently, and Grier's only reply was a slight inclination of his chin.

"I couldn't let Max kill you because of me. So... when Grier offered up a gun, I took it. If I was already dead then you would be alive, and you could help stop all the destruction that Max is causing. I put the gun to my head, and I pulled the trigger."

"It was empty," Grier explained before Kye could ask the question. "I needed to know that she loved you. That what we're doing for her, because of her, was worth it."

"That wasn't your call to make," Kye snapped.

"Yes, it was," Grier defended with raised eyebrows.

"You're not the only one with a stake in the game. A lot of us have had our hopes riding on you for years. We weren't going to get this close to blow it on someone who wasn't loyal to you. Turns out, she really does love you. Values your life above her own. She was ready to die for you, Kye. Just like the rest of us."

"The rest of you?" Kye asked as he sank onto the couch next to Eliana and wrapped an arm around her.

"Jez was here," Eliana said, looking up at him. "Turns out, she's not just good at covering bruises, she's good at faking them too. She put on some makeup, made it look like I'd been knocked around and my throat slit." Eliana pulled the collar of her shirt down to reveal the expertly applied gash in her throat. Touching it timidly, Kye could feel the prosthetic.

"Fuck," he breathed, raking a hand through his hair. "Then you sent the photo to Max's phone," Kye pieced together. Grier nodded.

"Told him she was like that when I got here," Grier added. "A little fake blood on the floor looked pretty convincing. We hoped it was anyway. You're alive, so it must have been."

"I was with Max when he got the picture," Kye informed them. "He was ecstatic when he thought I had done it. You… saved my life," Kye said and looked back to Eliana. "I would never be able to agree to kill you. I love you."

"I love you," she admitted softly and placed a hand on his cheek. She was still clearly rattled from her near death. Though the gun hadn't been loaded, she hadn't known that when she'd fired. Eliana was willing to kill herself to save him. Now here she was confessing her love for him. Kye dipped his head to give her a chaste kiss.

"Where's Jez now?" Kye asked when he noticed she wasn't anywhere to be found.

"She's gone," Grier said shortly. Kye looked at him with brows raised. "Packed a bag and hauled ass out of town. She's out, Kye. I guess this was her final act of charity."

"Where did she go? It's not going to be safe for her when Max finds out," Kye said.

"Jez can take care of herself. Right now the three of us need to figure out what our next move is. If I know anything, Max is going to want a body."

"He wants proof, that's for sure," Kye agreed. "I told him I'd send a video of Eli in the levee."

"The levee?" Grier asked harshly.

"I thought she was dead, Grier," Kye snapped back. "It was the first place I thought of. I knew if I headed that direction with her, there were at least two hospitals I could stop at."

"What's wrong with the levee?" Eliana asked, looking between the two of them.

"It's Max's property. It's where he stores all of his unwanted things," Grier said with an element of sarcasm.

"By that you mean…"

"Bodies," Kye finished. "Because of that, it's crawling with patrols, dogs, and cameras. Just in case any local cops decide to be a hero and crack down on Max's empire or any one of the demons, they won't risk a body turning up."

"So we won't go there," Eliana suggested. "The only levee in town is outside the lumberyard in the woods, any section of forest will do. Send a video of tossing me into a hole and that should buy us time. Right?" Clearly having something to put her mind toward was helping rid her of shock. Kye could see the wheels turning as she struggled to find a solution.

"We head just far enough in to trigger a few sensors, a few cameras, take the video and be gone. It could work," Grier agreed.

"We have to move fast. If we don't, Max will know we're plotting something," Kye said in a tense tone.

"If the place is monitored by cameras," Eliana said suddenly, "then how are we going to get in and out? You can dump me in the hole, but won't he see me climbing back out?"

"He doesn't have a camera on every tree," Kye said, standing. "We can take the Yukon. It has tinted windows. We dig a hole, fill a body bag with dirt, send enough video of you in the hole to satisfy him, then you get back inside, and we drive straight out of town. We won't stop until we reach the equator if necessary."

"You mean that?" Eliana asked, looking at Kye with hopeful eyes. "You're ready to leave all of this behind and come with me?"

"I'm done, Eli, I can't be a part of this. Not now that I know how twisted and sick things have gotten."

"So we leave those that are trapped to their fate?" Grier asked in anger. "We've worked for how long to overthrow Max from the inside just to tuck tail and run?"

"If we leave," Kye said looking from Grier back to Eliana, "can you put together a case against him?"

"Take him to court?"

"Have him arrested, thrown in jail, whatever it takes to stop him," Kye stated.

"I mean, I still have some of the paperwork from the cases he sent me. It doesn't directly incriminate him. You may need to testify."

"I can do that."

"Kye, that would likely mean that the State would bring charges against you too for aiding and abetting," Eliana explained as she rose to her feet and took his hands. "You'd be seen as an accomplice and co-conspirator."

"Whatever it takes to stop him," Kye emphasized.

"Let's take things one step at a time," Grier interrupted. "We need to get to the levee now. Too much time has passed already. Get your shit and get to the garage; I'll drive," Grier said and ducked out of the room.

"Hey," Kye said, grabbing Eliana's arm when she turned to get her things. He pulled her back against him and covered her mouth with his in a passionate kiss. "I thought I'd lost you. I really did... I thought you were..."

"I'm right here," she said, cutting him off and placing both hands on his face. "When I had that gun and I was ready to die, I just kept thinking, 'I hope Kye knows I love him'. Last time we spoke about that, I told you I didn't know if I could love you... but I was wrong. I do love you. So very much."

"I know," he said softly and gave her a brief kiss. "We're going to get through this. After tonight, it's all over. Just you and me."

"I want to believe that..."

"Believe it. Hold on to it. Let it keep you strong and hopeful," he encouraged, and she smiled softly.

"My dad..." she said as though she remembered something. "That night he shot you, do you remember?"

"Kind of hard to forget..."

"No, no, what I mean is, do you remember the van he

drove? How he'd stopped before he reached the checkpoint?"

"Yes."

"He was the one who discovered Max was transporting girls across state lines. Grier thinks Max has been trafficking women to Canada since before you even joined the club. If it hadn't been for my dad, who stopped because he heard them crying in the back, Max's operation may never have been found out."

"I remember Max grilled me about the contents of the van; it sounded like he was accusing me of stealing, but maybe what he wanted to know was if I'd seen the women captured. Or even set them free," Kye said, staring into the distance as he remembered the encounter. "Your dad was awful, but he had his redeeming qualities," Kye added.

"I know," Eliana said, parting from him long enough to pick up the shoebox from the couch. Opening the lid, Kye saw it was full of old photographs. "This is me as a baby," Eliana said, handing him the top one. "I thought all of these were gone, but Grier said he'd found them when he'd helped you clean out the house after I left."

"I told him not to throw anything away that might belong to you," Kye said, looking at the photo. It was an old Polaroid that was tinged yellow with age, but clearly showed Henry as a younger, thinner, and less intoxicated man holding a little bundle on his lap.

"Do you see this?" Eliana asked, pointing to where Henry's hand held her chubby baby one. Kye nodded. "My dad has his thumb pressed to my palm. When he was dying in the hospital, he took my hand like this. It was so forceful at the time I thought he was angry. Or he was panicked because he was suffocating. But now… I wonder if he just wanted to do this one more time. Have me wrap my fingers around his thumb and hold onto him like… like when I was a baby. When he was my whole world." Eliana was crying, and Kye took her in his arms.

"It's okay to love your dad and still be angry at him," Kye said as he pressed his lips against her hair. "Henry saved those girls who got away. It doesn't make up for anything he did to you and all the times he wasn't there, but you can know in your heart that Henry was a good person. And in his own way, he loved you very much." Eliana nodded and sniffled a few times before she was able to stop her tears.

"I know we don't have time for this…" she said, stuffing the picture into her pocket. "It's been a lot to take in today."

"We'll have all the time in the world to process these things and talk about them," Kye promised. "Get your bag and get to the garage. I have to get one of the suit bags from the closet upstairs. I've got a couple of black ones we can use as body bags."

"That's a terrifying thought," Eliana said, shivering. "Have you done that before? Used one to hide a body?"

"Eli…" he said cautiously, and she held a hand up.

"You're right, I don't want to know. I'll meet you in the car," she said and left the room. Kye made his way upstairs and retrieved the suit bags from the closet in his room and felt he might be sick. The last time he'd used one to conceal a body, he hadn't thought twice about it. Now he was going to be using one to conceal Eliana's body. Though she was very much alive, images of what he'd thought was her lifeless body in that photo would haunt him for years to come. He'd never forgive himself if that became a reality.

While he was still plenty angry at Grier for lying to him and almost killing the love of his life, he had to hand it to him; Grier's loyalty was unmatched, and it had been his quick thinking that had saved his life. Before the night was over, he'd save his life again too and Eliana's. Sighing one last time, Kye turned the lights off in the house that had once belonged to Eliana and that had become his home.

He knew the minute he shut the door behind him and climbed into the passenger seat of the Yukon SUV he'd never see her in that house again.

2

Eliana was shivering in the cold and in fright. She was watching helplessly as Kye and Grier dug her would-be grave. Their progress was illuminated by the headlights of the SUV but was still obscured by the downpour. They'd managed their way onto the property and just as the men had said, the forest was more of a compound. Once they'd passed through the chain-link fence, Eliana had searched the tree line frantically, looking through the tinted windows for cameras. It wasn't easy in the night, with the rain, through dark windows, but they'd managed to find a few. It was in the line of these cameras they were digging their hole.

Kye had been smart. He'd parked the SUV so the tailgate was slightly obscured and only half of the grave was within sight of the camera. This would ensure she could get in and out of the hole without being seen. Hopefully.

Eliana was pulled from her thoughts when Kye opened the door to the back. He was soaked from head to foot, and he had dirt smeared on his face. "Are you ready?" he asked. She climbed over the back of the seat to back where Kye tossed the shovel aside and unzipped the suit bag.

"Let's just get this over with," she said and lay down inside. Kye gave her an apologetic look before zipping it up. Before he fully encased her, he smeared a muddy hand over her face to help darken the bruises. Eliana took a steadying breath as he lifted her into his arms. Rain pattered the tarp-like material as soon as she was out of the back of the car.

"I'm recording," Grier said, and Kye nodded as he saw the cell phone Grier was pointing at them. Kye looked from the camera to the hole where he jumped inside and set the bag containing Eliana inside. Grier handed him the phone, and Kye had to wipe water from the lens to ensure it was visible when he unzipped the top to reveal Eliana's face.

Playing the part as best she could, Eliana remained motionless knowing she was being filmed. The next part was the scariest. Kye had loaded a gun with blanks and, while still filming, fired several rounds into the chest of the bag. The pellets were enough to tear holes and sting her skin, but not enough to puncture her.

The loud shots echoed through the air loud enough

to drown out the rolls of thunder in the distance. Kye hit send on the phone, and the video was off. He tossed it quickly to Grier and took hold of Eliana. "Come here," he said, drawing her out of the bag and into his arms. "It's over, it's over," he said quickly into her ear as she clung to him. He released her only long enough to jump out of the grave and hoist her up.

"Let's load up," Grier suggested and began filling the hole in.

"Get into some dry clothes; we'll take care of this," Kye said, holding the back door open for her. Eliana was grateful as she slid into the warm car and stripped of her now wet clothes. She had just tugged on pants and a shirt when she saw headlights approaching from the opposite direction. Giving the horn a quick honk, Kye and Grier looked up from their task. She pointed, and they turned simultaneously. Kye gestured for her to get down, and she was quick to lock the doors as she ducked in the back seat.

"Did Max send someone?" Kye asked, and Grier only shrugged. They watched as a tan Jeep pulled to a stop on the opposite side of the grave, and a single man exited. Wearing a green Park Ranger jacket, both Kye and Grier noted the handgun on his hip.

"What are you boys up to?" the middle-aged man wearing a broad-brimmed hat asked, his voice muddled by the rain.

"Digging a hole," Grier replied. The short, thin man circled, hands on hips, and spat into the hole as he neared them.

"Pretty big hole, you got something to bury?"

"Maybe we're looking for treasure."

"You looking to get that smartass shot, son?" the ranger asked, his annoyance was clear.

"We're not looking for trouble," Kye interjected before Grier could mouth off and cause a bigger problem. "We're just here to…"

"I know why you're here," he said sharply and removed the flashlight from his belt. "I have orders too, boys. My orders are to make sure you got the job done." He shined the light into the hole that was already half full of dirt. "She in there?"

"Yes," Kye answered. "We sent the video to Max."

"How'd you do it?"

"With a cell phone."

"You got a death wish, son?"

"Grier, shut up," Kye demanded. "I slit her throat. Put a couple in her chest to make sure she was dead. Sent proof to Max."

"Really? Seems like overkill to me," the ranger said shining the flashlight onto the car. Inside, Eliana ducked even lower to avoid the beam.

"Well, when Max wants proof…" Kye said, trailing off.

"Speaking of that," the ranger added as he pocketed his flashlight. "I need to see her."

"Fuck if I'm going to dig her back up," Grier snapped. "We've been out in the rain for an hour already. Max has his proof. You should have gotten here earlier."

"Then I'll do it." He picked up one of the discarded shovels and jumped into the hole.

"For fuck's sake, she's dead; just leave her be," Kye yelled. Behind the ranger's back, he gave Grier a worried look as the man began digging.

"I've got orders to deliver a hand," he called from inside the hole as he continued to dig. Grier gave Kye one last look, and he nodded. Trying to discreetly move backward, Kye used his large frame to block the hole from the view of the camera on the road.

"Let me help," Grier offered and jumped into the hole. The ranger didn't have time to argue as Grier pulled the knife from behind his back and drove it into the man's gut. His final scream was gurgled and mostly lost under the downpour, and a sudden flash of lightning gave Kye his chance. He was under the camera now and, using a rock from the ground, hit it dead center and hard enough to knock its position askew.

"Hurry!" Kye hollered. Grier set to the grisly task of separating the man's hand from his arm. Dragging his body out of the hole, he pushed it into the Jeep.

"We're fucked," Grier said, returning. He had blood on his right hand and a severed hand in his left.

"We need to go," Kye said just as quickly. The passenger door opened, and Eliana looked out. Her face was pale, and she couldn't tear her eyes away from the body part Grier was holding. "Come on," Kye said, helping her from the back and into the passenger seat. Grier rounded the front and slid into the driver's seat.

"Here," Grier said, reaching over Eliana to where Kye stood just outside her door. He handed him the ranger's cell phone.

"Please be unlocked," Kye prayed as he swiped the screen. Fortunately, the ranger hadn't set a password. Pulling up the text messages, he saw the unmarked number the ranger had been texting, the last one read: confirm that the girl is dead.

"What do we do?" Eliana asked as she read the message. Kye was already working, however.

'She's dead. Throat was slit and had a few bullet holes in her chest. Not much blood; she's been dead a while.' Kye sent.

"Nice touch," Grier complimented and set the hand on the dashboard. Eliana had to swallow the vomit that had risen in her throat. A moment of silence passed as they waited, and finally a response came in.

'Do you have the hand?'

'Yes, she doesn't need it anymore,' Kye punched in.

He hoped his brief impression of the ranger gave him the context of the man's dry sense of irony.

"They're going to want to see it," Grier spoke in a serious tone. Kye looked at him knowingly. As if on cue, the text came in.

'Send it back with the kid.'

"That's Max," Kye said, knowing that only the old man called him 'kid'.

"We're fucked," Grier said again and leaned back against the seat.

"No, you're not," Kye said, drawing both of their attention back. "You stick to the plan."

"Don't you mean 'we'?" Eliana asked, panic starting to creep up inside of her. Kye reached over her and buckled her seatbelt. "Kye?"

"Go," he said, but not to her. He was looking directly at Grier, their silent conversation taking place. Grier reached over, took the stump of a hand off the dash, and handed it to Kye over Eliana.

"You'll need this," he said and started the engine.

"Kye, no!" Eliana said and reached for her seat belt. He caught her arm and pulled her to look at him.

"I love you," he said desperately, eyes locked on hers. She was shaking her head, words lost in her throat. "I'm right behind you. I promise."

"Don't send me away again; don't do this," she pleaded. Memories of the time he'd shipped her off this way with her father. Now he was doing it again, but this time with a man who'd already stated he had no problem killing her.

"This time, I'm coming after you," he said, holding her face. He kissed her quickly, fiercely, and moved back to slam the door. Before she could protest again, Grier had gassed the engine, and they were speeding off, kicking up mud behind the tires.

* * *

KYE DID his best to clean himself up. Sitting in the ranger's jeep, he used rubbing-alcohol and gauze from the first aid kit to clean his face and hands. The body was stuffed in the trunk, and the grossly cut up appendage was on the seat next to him. Whether by fate or miracle, the short man had equally small hands, and although they were dirty, he hoped they looked petite enough to pass for a woman's. Eliana's to be precise.

Knowing he needed to swap out vehicles, it took him longer than he wanted to get back to the house and swap out the Jeep for his bike. He stashed the ranger's vehicle in the garage where it wouldn't be seen and collected the GPS. While inside, he stuffed the GPS, the cell phone, and Eliana's cell he'd taken from her bag when she wasn't paying attention, in the microwave and set the timer. The radiation was sure to kill any tracking devices that may be in place, not to mention any record of a signal.

Kye pulled his leather cut on, put the hand in a plastic bag, and brandished his helmet. Looking every bit the part of MC vice pres, he mounted his bike and sped off toward the clubhouse.

He could tell there was a full assembly. Riggs and his crew were causing mayhem at Jez's. Hamilton's usual crew were in the clubhouse drinking and cheering on a hockey game. Had circumstances been different, Kye would have been here right along with the rest of them. Now as he paced the clubhouse, watching with a feeling of dissidence, he felt like he was seeing the Screaming Demons with open eyes for the first time.

While most of the men seemed harmless, he could see the villains among them. They carried themselves like kings, their hands waving and beckoning for drink, food, or pussy. Kye could see the Wall Kats standing, waiting, their eyes dim and hollow. He'd never spent much time looking at them, but now he saw them. Truly saw them. Some looked like teenagers who'd gotten lost at the mall. Young and foolish and woefully unprepared for the world.

Then there were the others. Thin. Bruised. Staring at the ground while Demons monitored them. Hovered over them like pimps. In truth, that was likely what they were. How had he been so blind? How could he not have seen this? He'd been so singularly focused over the last ten years. Working to gain position and try in his own pathetic way to win Eliana over that he was completely ignorant of what was going on around him.

He'd built an empire on the backs of drug dealers, arms solicitors, and prostitution. Kye felt his stomach churning in knots. He'd thought part of him would be sad to leave the club, but at the moment he couldn't stand to be around any of it. The whooping and hollering from the men, the moaning and groaning from the clubhouse rooms, the smell of beer, cigarettes, and gasoline was repugnant to him.

He slammed the door to Max's office open without waiting for an invitation. To his shock, he saw Jez sitting on Max's lap on the couch. She cast him a fleeting look of feigned surprise, and Kye returned it.

"Ever heard of knocking," Max said coolly, and Jez subtly slipped off his lap and moved into the seat next to him.

"Here," Kye said, without waiting. He tossed the hand onto the table in front of Max and stood glaring. Max reached forward, but instead of retrieving the bag, he picked up his brandy glass before leaning back and sipping it. "Don't care to examine my handy work?"

"Is that meant to be a joke?" Max asked with a coughing laugh. Kye remained placid. "I know you put her in the hole," Max said, crossing his legs. "Damned if the rain didn't obscure the video you sent, but you did a good job of doing it within sight of the cameras. Very well thought out." Kye couldn't tell if his tone was patronizing or complimentary.

"Short of dragging her body in here, I didn't want to leave any room for doubt," Kye stated flatly. He wanted in and out and to be done with all of this. His contempt for the man in front of him tasted like vinegar in his mouth.

"You killed her?" Jez asked, playing her part well. Kye didn't know why she'd returned, but it was probably better that she did. Too many missing people and Max was going to catch on. "That brunette lawyer you brought through the bar?"

"Yes, he killed her," Max answered for him. "Strangled her, am I right?"

"I slit her throat, Max, you know that," Kye said with gritted teeth. Even the idea of it made Kye's eyes sting with tears.

"That's right," Max crooned. "How was that? Did she cry when she realized she'd been betrayed?"

"Yes," Kye said quietly, remembering Eliana's face when he'd sent her off again. "She cried and gagged on her own blood, and she died. If you don't mind, I've given you enough information and proof, and you can go fuck yourself with it."

"Ha!" Max bellowed, smile bright on his face. "That's

my boy." Max struggled to stand. He crossed to him and placed a hand on Kye's shoulder. "Good job, kid. You did a damn good job."

So he was convinced. Then why was there a gleam in his eye? Kye turned when he heard the door open. Dhal stood there with a grin on his face and a gun in his hand.

3

It was dawn before Eliana was allowed to sit up. Grier had ordered her to sit on the floor of the SUV all night as he drove. Knowing that, despite her reeling mind, she'd drifted in and out of sleep. Her restlessness had given way to haunting dreams of shallow graves, severed body parts, and seeing Kye's face in all of it. She had fleeting dreams of being chased by flocks of motorcycles and rattled in prison cells lined with paperwork. The droning nightmares ended when the car lurched, and she was jostled fully awake.

"Sorry," Grier said, though his tone conveyed no remorse as she rubbed her head where she'd slammed it on the underside of the glove compartment. Eliana struggled to stretch from her position on the floor. Her back ached, her legs were asleep, and her arms felt heavy at her side. To say nothing of the lump forming on her head where she'd just hit it. "You can get up," Grier said in the same flat tone.

"Thank God." She sighed as she slid into the passenger seat. The blood rushed to her legs, and they tingled like needle pricks all the way to her toes. "Where are we?" she asked, looking around her. The terrain was very different from the Atlantic Northeast where they'd come from. It was flatter, and though there was some greenery, it was hardly the deciduous terrain they'd left the night before. "I know we're going west," she observed when Grier didn't answer.

"Are we?" he asked in feigned ignorance. Eliana was too tired to roll her eyes, so she sighed instead.

"It's morning; the sun is rising behind us."

"Didn't know you were a boy scout," Grier commented.

"Doesn't take a genius to know the sun rises in the east, Grier," Eliana muttered. She fell silent, resting her sore head against the glass of the window. Signs flew past them on the road, but as they were on a rural high-way, none of the exit signs were very informative as to their location. Wherever they were, it was hours away from Kye.

As though remembering something, she turned in her seat and grabbed her backpack from the seat behind her. She was rummaging and fumbling through it, searching every pocket and crevice. Not finding what she was looking for, she upended it and scoured her belongings.

"I can't find my phone," she said, looking over at Grier. He'd kept his eyes trained on the road, one hand gripping the wheel, the other resting on the gear shifter. The SUV was an automatic, so she suspected he was used to driving a manual from his posture. "Grier?"

"What?"

"I can't find my phone."

"Did you look in your bag?"

"Are you trying to be funny or insufferable?" she asked, knowing full well he'd seen her sifting through her items for the last ten minutes.

"Are you laughing?"

"No."

"Then likely the latter."

"You know what, fuck you," she cursed and began stuffing her items haphazardly back into her bag.

"You're not my type."

"It wasn't really an offer," she snapped back. Turning her eyes to look back out the window, she struggled to replay the events of the night before. Though they'd planned as carefully as possible, it had all ended up feeling hastened and hurried. Things would have gone according to plan had the park ranger not shown up. But that was Max's play, wasn't it?

The last weeks in the confines of her former home,

doing Max's bidding, working to free guilty men under the guise of working off her debt had all felt like the final walk to the hangman's noose. Even in his weakened state, he'd been slowly tightening the rope; planning, plotting and blocking every escape from the ultimate trap he'd built. The park ranger had been the final installment. His insurance to make sure Kye had carried out his final order exactly.

"Have you heard from Kye?" She looked over at Grier. The man remained unmoving. He must have been a statue in a former life because he managed to sit so still, she couldn't tell if he was even blinking. "Stop ignoring me!"

"I'm not ignoring you. I'm not answering you," he replied.

"We can argue semantics, or you can just answer the question. Just tell me if you've heard from Kye. I don't have my phone. He might be trying to reach us." She was well aware of the pleading in her voice, but she made no attempt to stop it. Just shy of jumping out of the moving vehicle, she had no way of getting back to Kye outside of this man. Grier. Kye's best friend, supposedly. Yet he was entirely unhelpful to her.

"I haven't heard from him," Grier answered after a long moment of silence passed.

"Is that a bad thing?"

"It's not a good thing."

"The two of you, you have a plan; I know it," Eliana interjected.

"If you know, then why are you asking?"

"Stop it, just stop!" she shouted and banged her hand on the dashboard. "Pull over. I need air." When Grier didn't so much as let up on the gas, she unlocked the door and reached for the handle.

"What the hell?" he asked when she started to open the door. He slammed the brakes and pulled onto the shoulder of the two-lane highway. A cloud of dust settled around them as she jumped out and began pacing. Air was flowing freely in her lungs, but she still felt as though she couldn't breathe. Raising her arms to rest on the top of her head, she continued pacing and tried to steady herself with several long and deep breaths.

"Please, please just tell me," she begged when Grier exited the car and leaned against the hood. He was lighting a cigarette when she approached him. "I need to know. Please tell me we didn't just drive away and leave Kye to die. I have to know. Please, please tell me." She was crying now, and the stoicism in Grier was making it worse. If the night before had been the last time she'd ever see Kye, she'd never be able to forgive herself.

He'd taken the hand and gone to Max. She was certain of it. Maybe he thought they needed to buy time, maybe it was part of the plan; she didn't know. What she did know was that Kye had gone back into the snake's pit to try to keep her safe. If he died because of it, Eliana would have nothing to live for anymore. It would have been better if Grier had killed her, or loaded the gun he'd given her, or they had buried her in that pit and cut off a hand as proof.

"Kye and I have always had an escape plan," Grier said, letting out a long breath. "About six years ago, when the money really started rolling in, we put together an exit strategy in case we ever needed one. He has a fail-safe, and I have one."

"And that's where we're going now? His fail-safe?"

"Right now," Grier said, stomping out his cigarette, "we're just going. We're getting far away. That was the plan. We've made it far enough to put space between us and Max, but that's about it."

"So we find somewhere to hole up and wait for Kye. He said he was right behind us. He promised."

"That was twelve hours ago," Grier said, pinching the bridge of his nose. For the first time, she could see the tiredness on his otherwise handsome face. "We're not stopping anywhere."

"We're just going to drive then? Fine, where are we driving to?"

"Far away."

"How far?"

"Very far."

"Is there some magical reason you're not telling me where we're going?"

"Several, but the first of which is that you don't need to know," Grier answered harshly. "I'm going; you can either come with willingly or unwillingly."

"Unwillingly?"

"I promised Kye I'd get you there," Grier said, standing directly in front of her. "It might well be the last thing I promised him. I won't be made a liar of."

"Fine, but you can't drive the whole way. You said it's far, and you look like you're going to pass out you're so tired; at least let me drive some."

"No way in hell that's happening."

"I really, really don't like you," Eliana said with hands on her hips.

"That's good," Grier said, mimicking her posture. "The less you like me, the less you'll talk. Now, get back in the vehicle." She stared hard at him for a long moment wishing she could slap him. Instead, she resigned herself to shoot every ounce of anger and hatred into his damned green eyes that she could.

If... When Kye caught up to them, she'd be sure to tell him just how much she hated his best friend.

* * *

IT WAS NEARING dark before Grier pulled the car off the highway. The day had passed in a silent blur of road signs and roadkill. Now, as the SUV pulled into a truck stop for refueling, even the bright floodlights couldn't bring any clarity to her thoughts. There were only two trucks in the station, and they were both parked for the night. A small diner was attached to the gas station, but it was clearly closed already.

"Stay," Grier barked shortly before exiting the car. His voice was hoarse and gravelly. Though she was fuming at him, she sympathized with how tired he must have been. Now that it was dark, he'd been driving for twenty-four hours straight. Eliana had tried her best to track their movements, but as soon as she figured out where they were, they seemed to double back and take a different route.

As every hour passed, Grier's phone that had sat resting on the charger on the dashboard had remained quiet. There was no word from Kye whatsoever. Holding on to the slim hope that things were still going to plan was harder with each passing hour.

Fresh tears obscured her view of Grier as he finished fueling and made his way to the convenience store that was lit by neon lights. Her hand twitched toward the door handle, and she opened it. Stepping out into the night, her legs nearly buckled from lack of use. The air was thick and humid. Surely, they were farther south than she thought for the night to be this hot. She felt sweat mixing with her tears, and the salt made her suddenly thirsty.

Staring at the sparse cars that zipped by on the highway, she had a fleeting thought of stealing a car and making her way back to Pine Hill for Kye. But to what end? If Kye hadn't made it out, he was likely dead now, and she'd be signing her own death certificate by walking back into Max's domain. If Kye was alive, then he was on the road trying to catch them, or meet them, or whatever the hell the plan was. With a hand pressed to her throat and the other over her stomach, Eliana stifled her panic. She was so fed up with feeling trapped.

Pacing like a caged lion, even her feet couldn't figure out where they wanted to go. First toward the convenience store, then back to the SUV, then in no particular direction; she was wandering the parking lot that smelled of gasoline and burning rubber. Squeezing her eyes shut, her mind conjured images of Kye. How desperate he'd looked when he buckled her into the vehicle. Sent her away. Again.

Her enraged cry tore open the night, and she fell to her knees. Screaming a second time, anger seeped out of her like sweat. How could he do this her? The worst night of her life had been the first time he'd sent her away, and now he'd done it again. She felt like the body of a yo-yo, always being tugged and flung in whatever direction the wielder chose. Always dangling by a thread. Never having any say in where she went.

Not this time.

"Hey!" she called to a trucker sitting in his cab. He was reading a newspaper and drinking something out of a Styrofoam cup. He looked up when she approached his vehicle. In his late forties to early fifties, he had a full beard and a round belly he kept his hands propped on. "Can I get a ride?"

"Where to?" he asked, sitting a little straighter.

"Anywhere," she replied with wide eyes.

"I'm headed to Wisconsin before the morning."

"That's fine, drop me anywhere; I just need to get out of here," she said hurriedly.

"You running from something?" he asked, turning to look at her more fully. "Or someone?"

"No, no. I won't bring any trouble on you. I just have to get out of here."

"Alright then, miss, hop in." Eliana didn't wait for a second invitation before she began rounding the trailer. She saw Grier exiting the store with bags in his hands, and she moved quicker. It was too late, though, as he spotted her.

"What the hell are you doing?" he yelled and sprinted across the parking lot toward her. Eliana was climbing into the truck when he caught her. "Get out of there!"

"No! I'm not going to sit in a vehicle with you a moment longer."

"So you're going to sit in a truck with him?" Grier asked, gesturing to the very confused looking man. She remained silent but adverted her eyes. "What about Kye? Hmm?"

"What about him? He hasn't sent any word. He's probably dead!"

"Yeah, he probably is!" Grier yelled in an uncharacteristic level of emotion. She'd not suspected he was capable of this level of emotion based on his usual monotone behavior toward her. "So you're going to tell me he died in vain? He sent himself to his grave, buying us time to escape, so you can drive off with this fucking Santa-Claus-looking motherfucker?"

"That's it, get out!" the trucker yelled. When Eliana didn't move fast enough, he reached for the gun under his seat. She practically flung herself out of the cab. She shoved past Grier and began walking away from him in no particular direction.

"Get back here," Grier said, grabbing her arm. She yanked it away from him then reared back and slapped him hard across the face. The crack was sickening, but Grier didn't so much as flinch.

"I hate you!" she screamed. Still, Grier didn't make the slightest movement. She slapped his chest, and when he remained silent still, she began hitting him repeatedly. "I hate you and I hate him! I hate Kye. I hate him!" Her body fell weak with sobs, and when she lost her strength to hit Grier anymore, one of his arms wrapped around her shoulders and pulled her against his warm chest. "He left me again. He sent me away. I hate him. I hate him!" She wept as her arms wove around his torso.

"I know," Grier murmured, resting his chin on her head. "I hate him too."

4

Just before dawn the next morning, Grier pulled the SUV onto another highway exit. This was no truck stop; however, it was a small town. Resembling most small towns, Eliana ticked off the usual staples: a steepled church, a couple of motels, a bar, a consignment shop, and a café. It was like every small-town architect used the same blueprints. She could almost guess what would be around every corner based on the town she'd grown up in. Even the people looked typical.

Early morning pedestrians were flocking to the streets. It must have been Sunday due to the well-dressed individuals who were walking toward the church. Little girls in cute dresses stood safely between modestly dressed women and men in button-down shirts. Eliana wracked her brain. She felt so disoriented, had it not been for the guide of the churchgoers, she wouldn't have been able to tell what day of the week it was had her life depended on it. All of her days rolled together like one long blur. Come to think of it, other than the snacks from the gas station, she couldn't remember the last time she'd eaten.

"What are we doing here?" she asked when Grier drove through town and pulled onto a dirt road. Since her meltdown at the truck stop, their relationship had hardly become more sociable, but there seemed to be a quiet understanding that passed between them. Grier was Kye's best friend. Eliana was Kye's true love. Their affection for the man united them, and at the present, their mutual hatred and anger at him bonded them.

Eliana felt ashamed of herself for being so selfish. Since their departure, she'd only been thinking of her own suffering and misery without Kye. Not knowing if he was dead, alive, or something in between. She hadn't stopped to think that Grier was grieving too. Not knowing anything about the man, she hadn't realized he'd been expressing his pain through silence and determination. He'd torn through a third of the country in just under two days, trying to keep them safe, making sure there was no one tailing them. No one could follow them. In days of modern speed cameras and surveillance, especially anywhere within the proximity of state borders, he had to make sure he didn't trip any sensors. If he did he was seen driving in and out repeatedly to throw anyone off the trail.

It was meticulous work, and the more she observed his driving and spent less time brooding she could appreciate his mastery. Especially running on Snickers bars and energy drinks for the last thirty-six hours. Grier was a warrior from the top of his head to the tip of his toes. Even now as she stared at his profile, she felt a new appreciation for him. Though he still scared her, unnerved her, and Lord knows annoyed the hell out of her with his silence, he'd rescued her. They were free from Max's reach. At least for the time being.

"It's an old storehouse," Grier answered when they reached the end of the dirt road. An abandoned house sat at the end of the long driveway. Based on the peeling shingles, broken windows, and hinged doors the house hadn't been used in years. Before she had the chance to ask how on earth this rundown foreclosure could serve any purpose, Grier turned sharply and drove to the back of the house and across a short field toward a barn.

The red paint was now tinged orange from age, but it looked otherwise unfazed with time. There was only a single round window toward the top of the structure, and there was a chain bolt on the door. Grier pulled the SUV to a stop next to the barn and killed the engine.

"What did you store here?" she asked and followed him as he exited the SUV. "Ghosts?" she asked sarcastically, and when she stepped on the remnants of a broken fence, she kicked a plank that housed several rusty nails. "Tetanus?"

"And scurvy," Grier chided. He used a set of deadbolt cutters that had been hidden in the bushes to break the lock on the door. The chain rattled to the ground, and he tossed the cutters aside before he flung the doors to the barn wide open. The only light in the barn was a single bare bulb that Grier turned on via the small switch chain that hung beside it. Not that it did much good. However, the open barn doors were more than adequate to illuminate the fortress inside.

Eliana gaped as she saw the inside of the building. It was meticulously organized save for the wooden planked floors underfoot. The walls to her right were lined with gun racks that held everything from handguns to assault weapons and what she was pretty sure was a bazooka. All hung perfectly on pegs; she wouldn't have been surprised if they were alphabetized. The tool chests on the far wall held containers of ammunition and medical supplies.

Grier moved about the room as though he'd been here several times before. He was soon out of her sight as the center of the room was occupied by a large structure she assumed was a concealed vehicle under a gray tarp based on the shape of it. Having no desire to see the guns any more closely, she moved instead to the left side where the wall to her left was lined with a long map of the US.

It looked as though someone had charted several routes and circled a few key locations, Pine Hill being one of them. What she saw seemed more of a battle strategy than a road trip map. On the right side was a list of locations— cities, the names of roads, or possibly even hotels or buildings. Between the colored pegs were strings of matching colors that possibly guided the reader. Her eyes moved over it quickly, her mind eager to have any bit of information to devour. Two days with nothing to do but stare out the window and a veritable mannequin to talk to, she was starved for stimulation.

"So…" she said, trailing off as she surveyed the map that was lined with colored pins. Her eyes darted back and forth as though reading it like a textbook. "We're in Kentucky."

"What makes you think that?" Grier asked as he put an empty duffle bag on the table and began filling it with items he'd gathered from around the room.

"This pin is red," she said, pointing to the one pinned on the state of Kentucky. "The ones in the north are green and the ones in the south are yellow."

"So."

"So, this is the only red one. As in… 'you are standing here' kind of red," she stated as she explained her line of reasoning. "We're in Kentucky."

"If you say so," Grier muttered as he continued in his task without looking at her.

"Why won't you tell me where we are? Is it so difficult to tell me? I don't see the harm in it."

"If you're clever enough to figure out the map, you should be clever enough to decipher why I won't tell you," Grier replied.

"As far as I can tell your only reason for not telling me is because it annoys the hell out of me, and that seems to be your favorite pastime," Eliana bit.

"See?" Grier paused in his packing to glance at her. "You're clever."

"Wait," she called as he moved to the center of the room and began drawing back the tarp that covered a large vehicle. It was a milky white Hummer with even darker windows than the Yukon and steel rims. "The only reason you're not telling me our exact location is that it annoys me? You're that committed to pissing me off?" Her ire was rising quicker than her blood pressure. Zipping the bag he'd been filling, he looked squarely at her again.

"Yeah," he said nonchalantly.

"Are you kidding me?"

"No."

"What the hell is your problem?" Eliana snapped, placing her hands firmly on her hips. "This obviously isn't easy on either of us, so why do you seem set on punishing me? You're deliberately making things harder on me."

"Yeah, I am," Grier admitted with a shrug.

"Why?"

"Why?"

"Yes, why?"

"Because you've been a massive pain in the ass ever since you arrived!" he hollered. Turning to face her fully, Grier crossed his arms to glare down at her.

"I'm the pain in the ass? You've barely said ten words since we fled Pine Hill."

"Ever heard the old adage, 'if you don't have anything nice to say, don't say anything at all?'"

"Of course."

"That's what I'm doing. I'm saying nothing at all because I don't have anything nice to say to you!"

"What did I do?"

"You… you…"

"What? What did I do?" Her voice was shrill, and if she didn't take a moment to steady herself, she was going to slap him again. Based on the fire burning behind Grier's emerald green eyes, she wasn't altogether certain he wouldn't hit her back this time.

"You're the reason Kye isn't here! You're the reason he's probably dead!"

So, there it was. The reason for his animosity. The

reason he hated her. Grier blamed her for the situation they were in.

"That's not fair, and you know it."

"Right about now, I don't particularly care what you think is fair," he said flatly. "This exit strategy was meant to be for three, but because Kye can't keep his head straight when it comes to you; now it's just us. Rather than going out, guns blazing at his side, I'm stuck playing babysitter for you."

"I didn't ask you to!"

"No, but Kye did."

"And you obey his every word? Like what, a sidekick? His pet? Are you in love with him or something?" A short scream caught in her throat when he lunged forward. Grabbing her arm painfully, he lifted his hand to back-hand her. She cowered and lifted her hands to protect herself. When the blow didn't come, her eyes peered open. Grier remained in striking position, breathing hotly through his nose and making his nostrils flare.

"This is your one warning," he said through clenched teeth. He released her, and Eliana's hand flew to her upper arm that throbbed where he'd held her. Grier turned his back and placed both hands on the table. The muscles in his back rippled under his shirt with every shaky breath. "Yes, I love him," Grier said quietly, dangerously.

"Oh…" Eliana said, feeling very self-conscious suddenly. Grier remained in the same stance but turned his head to give her a sideways glance.

"I love Kye like a brother," he elaborated. "He's the only family that I've ever known. He's saved my life more times than I can count. He's kept me clean while in the club and had my back just like I've had his. We have a bond. One that you'll never understand."

"Try me," she said with arms crossed. Not in an impertinent manner, but more out of desperation. At this moment, despite what they both wanted, they only had each other, and Eliana felt a burning need to make Grier at least be civil with her. The only way to do that was to understand him better, and since this was the first time he'd spoken more than five words together, she was hoping to piggy-back on his streak.

"You don't know what an MC club is until you're in one. Every day its blood and balls," Grier started, still leaning over the table. "Bonds of brotherhood are forged amid high speeds and shootouts. I was a Demon for nearly a year before Kye came along. It was brutal. Ugly. The hardest thing I'd ever done. I didn't have the luxury of a family that cared for me, and until Kye came along, I didn't have anyone watching my back in the club the way he has."

"You were initiated, they accepted you. Surely someone…"

"I was good at what I did. I can drive. I can shoot. I was an asset. A soldier. Nothing more. Certainly not to Max," Grier said with the faintest hint of disappointment in his voice. "The night we went on our first run together was the night your dad shot him. No one had my back that night. They left me on the bridge to face gunfire on my own. Not Kye. He came back for me. Gave me the credit for recovering the van. He put others before himself, and that saved my neck. That was just the first of a million times. You don't spend day after day in the trenches with someone and not get close. I'd die for that man."

"So would I," Eliana said, holding his gaze. To her surprise, after a long moment, Grier was the first to look away. "Kye was always putting others first?" Grier nodded. "That's what he's doing now. I didn't ask for this. If I'd known how things were going to happen, I would have let you bury me in that hole. Kye made his choice. He made it for me… and for you. I'm sorry for all of this."

"You should be," Grier said, and Eliana looked surprised. That was until a soft grin tugged at the corner of his mouth. She left out a puff of air and rolled her eyes.

"We don't know that he's dead."

"No, and we may never know," Grier said, standing upright and shouldering the stuffed bag on the table.

"I meant, he could be alive," she said and watched as he unlocked the Hummer and tossed the duffle into the back.

"Yes," Grier agreed. "He could be. Which means we have to get on the road. Kye and I both had our routes planned if we ever needed an escape. I can't deviate, and if he's on the move neither will he."

"I get the haste, I understand you're retracing routes to cover our tracks, avoiding major freeways, cities, and crossings, but to what end?" she asked when she saw him open the back and toss in a couple of sleeping bags. When Grier didn't answer, she huffed. He sighed as well and rest his arm on the open door. They needed to come to a better arrangement than arguing every time the car stopped. Mostly because Grier was too tired to continue this maddening soap opera with her.

"Belize," he said in a tone of finality. "We're going to Belize."

$\mathcal{K}$ye was startled awake by the sharp smack across his face. He hated his reaction, but the gasp and moan couldn't be helped. His hands were tied together and drawn upward over his head where they were secured to the exposed sewer pipe. The room he'd been in for the last day, or possibly two, was barely a storage room. The cement enclosed room was in the basement of the clubhouse. He'd been able to discern that much at least.

Dhal, who was currently wailing on him with his fists, was all pomp and show. He acted so high and mighty, but at the core, he was a bully and a thug with a crusty exterior and a soft underbelly. Having hooded him and pistol-whipped him on the floor of Max's office, Kye had feigned unconsciousness long enough to decipher where he was being taken. He'd need to know where he was so when he inevitably escaped his bonds, he could get the hell out of the clubhouse as fast as possible.

"You ready to talk?" Dhal asked as he wiped the blood from his knuckles with the bottom of Kye's shirt. "Max wants to know where your little girlfriend is. He knows she isn't dead."

"She's not? That's news to me," Kye croaked out with a dry throat. He hadn't had so much as a drop of water since he was taken below. He couldn't be sure how much time had passed as there were no windows. There was no rhyme or reason when the door would open or close. Kye was no stranger to torture. He'd done it many times himself to others, so he was sure to keep his mind occupied during the down time and dissociated during the beatings. Based on the wild look on Dhal's face, he was due for another one.

"It was a cute ploy, but Max isn't stupid. None of us believed you had the balls to kill her. You're a fucking waste of space and a poor excuse for a man. Since she's not anywhere to be found in town, we need to know where she's going, which direction she went, and who might be helping her. Besides your butt-buddy, Grier, that is. So, I ask again. Are you ready to talk?" He cracked his knuckles pretentiously. "Please," Dhal continued before Kye could answer, "please don't be. I am getting so much satisfaction out of beating the shit out of you."

"I can tell," Kye said, spitting blood on the floor. "What are you going to do next? Jerk off while you make me moan your name?" Another hard punch to the gut made Kye dry heave. He wouldn't admit it, but his chest was on fire, and he couldn't feel his arms anymore.

"You're pathetic," Dhal crooned in his gravelly voice as he took a seat in the single chair that sat opposite where Kye dangled. "I bet you think yourself a hero, but you're not; you're pathetic. All this," he said, gesturing with his hands, "for some woman. Not even a very pretty one."

"Pretty enough," Kye said, trying to get his feet under him. When he hung from his arms with his full weight, he found it was almost impossible to breathe.

"To fuck? I suppose," Dhal agreed, crossing one leg over the other, "but pretty enough to be tortured? Lose status and rank within the club? Not hardly. If I was you, had things handed to me the way they were handed to you… I'd never lose my presidency for some dried-out pussy."

"Then it's a good thing you're not me," Kye stated. "Although you spend an awfully long time trying to be." Dhal's eyes narrowed. "Sure, you conned and schemed your way into the club, took your oath, and garnered favor to be put on Max's private security thinking it was giving you a position of authority, but no one gives two shits about you, Dhal."

"Shut up, I earned my patches same as everybody else!"

"Did you?" Kye asked with a cough he disguised as a laugh. "You act so badass… You know, I shouldn't admit this," he said, looking at Dhal with amusement, "I looked you up three years ago when you joined." A muscle in Dhal's jaw twitched. "Yeah, you came in here spitting stories about your days in the military, how tough and badass you are, how brave and fierce and noble you were defending our country…" The chair fell over when Dhal stood abruptly. "How amusing it was to find you never saw active duty. What was the record? Mentally unstable for combat?"

"That was one report, and it didn't stop me from joining a clandestine unit after I was discharged! I've seen warfare!"

"Dishonorable Discharge," Kye continued. He was smirking, and it made his dry lips crack and bleed.

"For fighting with a self-righteous officer, tried to tell me how to do my job, so it came to fists."

"Yeah, I'm sure she put up a good fight." Kye could see the next blow coming in time to turn his jaw and deflect most of it. When Dhal raised his hand again, Kye burst out laughing, and it made him stop. "Look at you! So tough and badass… beating women and men who are tied up. Let's all quake in fear of the great Dhal who earned his participants patches like a fucking Girl Scout selling cookies."

"Fuck you!"

"Not tonight, honey; I have a headache." Despite his attempts to keep a jovial mood, when Dhal went at him again with his fists, Kye couldn't keep a thought inside outside of the pain. His already bruised ribs were cracking, his head was bleeding, and the lack of food and water was taking its toll. He couldn't stop himself from losing consciousness.

THEIR NEXT NIGHT on the road, Grier had finally succumbed to exhaustion. Now, while it was dark, he pulled to the back of another truck stop somewhere in Tennessee. When the back seats were down, they unrolled sleeping bags, and before Grier even climbed into his, he was passed out.

Knowing she only had a small window of opportunity, Eliana grabbed her bag and quietly exited the vehicle. Abutting the gas station was the standard convenience store, but this one also housed a twenty-four-hour diner. It was nearly vacant when she stepped inside, and the bell above the door rang delicately. The waft of diner-quality food smelled especially fragrant considering her last several meals had come out of a fast-food bag.

When she was seated and had ordered a coffee and dessert, she pulled her laptop out of her bag and plugged it in. Firing it to life, Eliana quickly pulled up her social media accounts and checked her emails, hoping to find any contact from Kye. There was nothing.

Pulling up the application that tracked her phone's location, she was met with a message that read 'no signal found'. Although frustrated, she wasn't exactly surprised. She'd long suspected that Kye or Grier had taken her phone and smashed it, burned it or tossed it in the bathtub. Whatever it took to kill the signal. Even Grier was using a burner phone that he kept charging in the SUV. Though she didn't know why. She never saw him using it or even checking it. So many times she'd wanted to reach over and try to find Kye's number and call him. He must have read her thoughts at some point because out of the blue that afternoon he'd informed her that there were no numbers stored in the phone, and she wouldn't be able to call anyone.

When the coffee came, Eliana was grateful for something to sip on. Hell, she was grateful to be out of the car. She was almost sure she was going to have sores on her ass from sitting so long, and she desperately needed a shower and a full meal. Without being able to resist, she pulled up the old records from Pine Hill. Having used this work computer to help her build defenses for criminals Max wanted free, there were still some documents available for her reading.

Most of it was useless jargon. Judicial loopholes she'd been able to exploit in her favor, but some of it was useful. While not directly incriminating, she wondered if any of it could be salvaged to trace back to Max or the MC. With nothing else to occupy her mind, she began reading and rereading everything she had stored. While she'd spent her youth loving everything about the courtroom, laws, and the art form of its interpretation, she now held a disdain for it. She'd seen firsthand how a murderer could walk free simply because an arresting officer didn't say the exact right thing. It was sick.

Vowing at that moment, if she lived and they managed to get across the border to freedom, she swore to find a better way to work in the law. When she'd first decided to become a defense attorney she thought it would be to defend those who couldn't or were unable to defend themselves. Now she realized the position was too fragile. You couldn't always tell the bad guys from the good guys, and even if you could, it didn't mean justice was served. Look at her present situation.

Max was a bad guy. His cronies were bad men. The criminals he'd sent her casefiles on were certainly bad men. And all of them were walking free. They didn't have to worry about being held prisoner or spend their days looking over their shoulders. They could go anywhere they pleased. Do anything they wanted. They were free to commit the same crimes all over again.

Whereas Eliana, who believed herself to be a relatively good person, had spent the last couple of months entirely in captivity. While not a jail cell per se, it might as well have been. First, she'd been locked in her childhood home facing demons and ghosts of her past, and now she was, at times, quite literally locked in a vehicle. She wasn't free to go anywhere and even if she didn't manage to ditch Grier, she'd spend the rest of her life looking over her shoulder. If Kye had failed their rouse, Max would never stop hunting her. Even dead, he'd find a way. She was sure of it.

No. She didn't want any part of the song and dance that came with being a defense attorney anymore. Grier had told her they were going to Belize. Maybe there was something she could do there? Work with locals… Hell, what was she thinking? She'd never work in law again.

Sighing, she closed the lid to her laptop and pinched the bridge of her nose. She felt weary straight through to her bones. She missed Kye. He had this way of making everything seem better just by being in the room. If he was dead, she wouldn't rest until she'd brought down every single Screaming Demon and personally locked them in cages. The local authorities might be on their payroll, most were likely too afraid to stand up to the club, but she wasn't afraid anymore. She'd burn the place down if necessary.

What could she do from Belize? If that was really where they were going. Part of her didn't believe it. Wasn't it more likely Grier was playing another prank on her? He seemed to find a level of amusement in keeping her disoriented. Maybe it was revenge for her part in getting them in this mess, or maybe it was his personality to play the trickster. She hadn't figured that out yet.

The possibility of going to Belize again, especially after so much agony the last several months, seemed euphoric. Her second summer at Harvard she'd gone to Belize over spring break with her girlfriends. Lyndsey's uncle was an international pilot, and he'd hooked them up with his timeshare. It was a beautiful cabana nestled right along a public section of beach. The city had been alive with tourists when she was there, and the whole week had been nonstop sunshine, mojitos, and wide-open ocean.

Eliana found herself smiling at the memory. She could hardly remember what it was like to be so carefree, but it seemed just a little bit closer at the moment. It had taken some convincing from her friends to get her to go out dancing their second night there, but Eliana remembered the red dress she'd worn and how she'd danced until her flipflop broke. She could still hear the laughter and the samba music that had resounded from the four-man band. They'd stayed at a bonfire all night until the sun came up and had to sleep until noon.

Eliana's eyes snapped open. She remembered something. When she'd been at the beach club where there was music and dancing, she'd seen something. Although admittedly slightly inebriated at the time, she'd still been triggered into a memory. When she and Lyndsey had gone to the bathroom together, they'd had to use a portable restroom outside and walked past a long line of parked Vespas and mopeds. Among them had been a Harley Davidson with chopper handles. Even at the time, Eliana had thought it unusual. She doubted any of the patrons in Belize could afford the expensive motorcycle, let alone leave it parked in the open.

As she'd stared at it, Eliana's mind had wandered back to Kye and his stupid motorcycle club. The sight of it and the memory of her former boyfriend had put her into a slightly depressed mood she'd then buried under two more alcoholic beverages. Never having confided in Lyndsey who Kye was, not for a few more years anyway, she hadn't said anything.

Now, looking back, Eliana wondered… had it been Kye there in Belize? He'd admitted to keeping tabs on her. Even Max had said Kye made regular trips down to Cambridge over the years to check up on her. Had Kye known she was going on that trip? Had he followed her to Belize? The idea of it made her head swim. Her spring vacation there had been, and still was, one of the happiest times of her life. Now it seemed more than ironic they were headed back that direction.

She wouldn't put it past Kye to orchestrate this entire thing. That was the way he was. Always in the rafters, always behind the scenes pulling strings and guiding her life like some puppet master or guardian angel. In her heart, she'd wanted to return to the beautiful, warm location. Was there going there now a final act of kindness from Kye? Had he done his best to secure her happiness by sending her here?

More importantly… how could she ever be happy in beautiful Belize without Kye?

---

6

*E*liana's hair was tinged with gold as she lay sprawled on her stomach in the sunshine. In the distance, she could hear the rush of the ocean. Waves lapped at the shore, and seagulls cawed in a soothing manner. Her skin was kissed bronze with tan, and her eyes were blissfully closed. Lying with her back to him, he trailed a finger along the bare skin. It was warm to his touch, but he saw her shiver and small goosebumps appear. Her white bikini stood in contrast against her flushed skin, and she rolled her head to face him. Eyes still closed, she smiled.

He leaned forward and caught her mouth in a sweet kiss. Yet the moment he pulled away, she grabbed him by the back of the neck and rolled him on top of her to deepen the embrace. The feel of her underneath him made him hard. Her body seemed equally receptive as she snaked her legs around his waist. Her moans in his mouth sent shockwaves of desire through him, and he couldn't stop himself from grinding against her. The feel of the sand beneath his hands and her writhing body was bliss. Pure bliss.

"Come on now, wake up." A splash of cold water on his face was more welcome than a slap, but being pulled from his exquisite dream sure felt like one. Opening his eyes, he saw Max standing in front of him.

"I prefer Dhal," he croaked, and Max grinned.

"I hear you two have been spending a lot of time together," Max noted as he spun the metal chair around and straddled it. Draping his hands over the back, Max stared at him for a long, quiet moment. Kye did his best to meet his eyes, but he could hardly keep his feet underneath him, and either his right eye was swollen shut or it had fallen out. Kye wasn't quite sure.

"Well, you know, never too late to make a new friend," Kye managed to say. The pipe over his head had been leaking for the last several hours, and the filthy water that dripped from it made the cement floor slick.

"A smartass to the last," Max observed with a chuckle. "I'd be proud if I wasn't so damn disappointed in you."

"I could say the same for you, Max," Kye said and gave up trying to stand. He settled for dangling, his shoulders popping painfully in their sockets.

"How is that?" Max asked, folding his hands.

"You let me down too," Kye began. "I've done every-thing you ever asked. Without question and usually better than expected, I've served at your side and built your empire. Have I not?"

"You have," Max agreed.

"I never took more than my share of a cut, kept away from booze, drugs, and I haven't had a single run-in with the law that you've had to bail me out of."

"You've been good," Max said, nodding. "You've been damn good. What's your point?"

"I never asked you for anything," Kye said and licked his dry lips. "Why couldn't you let me have her? After everything... why couldn't you just let me have her?" Kye was frustrated at his own show of emotion, but he didn't bother exerting the effort to stifle it. He was too dehydrated for tears, but the ache in his voice was evident.

"Do you remember what I told you when you first joined?" Max asked and stood.

"Don't stick your dick in a dirty tailpipe?" Max barked out a laugh and knocked once on the only door to the room. It opened, and Max accepted a pitcher of water and two glasses. Kye felt his throat go even dryer as Max poured himself a drink of water and sipped on it.

"True, I did say that," Max said with laughter still in

his voice. "What I also told you was to always put the club first."

"I've done that…"

"No, you haven't," Max said, pouring a second glass of water and setting it on the chair. He crossed to Kye and untied the rope keeping his hands above him. Despite Max's weakened condition, he was still strong enough to hold Kye up and help ease him to a sitting position on the floor. For the first time in days, Kye felt circulation in his arms and hands, and they burned painfully. "You've done well for the club, made us a lot of money, but you've always had ulterior motives. Selfish motives."

"Have I?" Kye asked and his arms shook as Max handed him the glass of water which Kye downed so quickly he choked on it.

"Easy now," Max said gently and poured him another cup of water. "I've watched you carefully, son, for a long time. You were a good soldier. Smart as hell, a lot more clever than a room full of my best men. I relied on you. I'm not too proud to say I depended on you. But while you served me with your left hand, your right hand was always hidden. Always stashing away and holding on to something else."

"Eliana," Kye admitted, and Max nodded.

"Your loyalty has always been divided. I know you've held on to the notion that you could make it all work.

You could run the Demons and have your woman. I don't know why you never made the move, maybe you were waiting for me to kick the bucket, but part of you felt you needed to be MC president before you'd earned her."

"Maybe it was my penance," Kye said as he sipped the water more slowly. The cool water soothed his burning throat, and the glass edge rattled between his teeth.

"Maybe," Max said squatting in front of him. "Maybe I just didn't die fast enough for you." Kye grinned. "Whatever the reason, I've known all along that this decision was going to make or break you. I had hoped that enough Demon blood ran through your veins that you'd see there was more value in what we'd built here than in some girl, but I was wrong. You chose her over your brothers. You chose her over me."

"I tried to choose both," Kye said, meeting Max's eyes.

"You can't have both."

"Now I have neither," Kye said, and Max gave him a soft smile.

"Now you have neither," he agreed. "Where is she, Kye?" Max asked directly. "I know she's not dead. We dug up the grave and found an empty bag. The park ranger on my payroll is rotting in your garage and is conveniently missing a hand."

"What a coincidence," Kye breathed on an exhale.

Max set his jaw firmly and stood. He moved back to the chair and withdrew a large Bowie knife from his belt. Though the dank room was dark, the glint of metal still caught his eyes.

"You're tough, and you've got balls the size of globes, no one is going to deny you that, but if you don't tell me where she is then I am going to kill you today," Max said firmly. His voice returned to its usual cold, gravelly bray. His eyes looked like two steel orbs in the dim lighting and the rigidity of his posture left no room for doubt. Max was going to kill him.

"I don't know where she is, Max," Kye admitted and set his glass on the ground next to him. "I put her in a car and sent her away. Her cell phone and the GPS in the vehicle are fried. I made sure there was no way to know where she is. I figured, if it came to torture, it was best I not know."

"That's noble," Max complimented, but his tone conveyed his annoyance. "You may not know where she is, but you know where she's going. You haven't been in love with her all these years to lose her now. Tell me where she's going."

"Max…" Kye said, looking up at the man. "Look at where we are. You say I've had divided loyalty. Does it look like I'm divided now?" Max turned his back as he picked up his glass of water.

"No, son," Max said with the beginning of tears in

his eyes. He drank the last of his water before setting the glass down and brandishing his knife. "You've made your decision finally. I hate that it's come to this."

"Me too," Kye said softly. A fleeting silence passed where both men allowed themselves to feel the grief of the loss they were experiencing. Though opposite sides, they were still the same coin. Kye pressed his back against the wall and slowly stood.

"Let's be done with this," Max whispered to himself. He turned much quicker than his age and infirmity would give the impression. The blade of the knife sliced through the air, but rather than meeting Kye's flesh, it hit the stone wall.

Kye, not nearly as debilitated as he'd allowed Max to think, had ducked the blow and while Max was off-balance, Kye tackled him straight into the chair. They clattered noisily to the floor, and Max grunted from the blow. He lifted the knife, and it nicked Kye's chest, but before it could pierce him fully, Kye grabbed Max's wrist and wrenched it so hard that the bones cracked together, and he dropped the blade.

"No!" Max groaned as Kye punched him. He crawled toward the knife, almost cutting his hands on the broken glass from the cup that had shattered. Max took his opening and struck Kye in the kidney with his fist. White-hot pain seared through his side, and the breath left his body. "I'll fucking kill you," Max growled and scrambled after the knife.

"Not today," Kye snapped. Grabbing the shard of glass from the floor, he stabbed at the only part of Max he could reach. The glass sliced through Max's cheek, and when the old man screamed in pain, Kye drove the sharp end into his eye. Blood splattered on Kye's hands and forearms, and the sickening squish of flesh being mutilated mixed with Max's horrified shouts.

Kye kicked Max in the chest and flew to his feet. Retrieving the knife, the door banged open behind him. Kye turned to see a startled Dhal in the doorway. Dhal looked from Max's motionless body on the floor to Kye. He grinned realizing he was now free to kill him.

"You should have drawn sooner," Kye said when Dhal reached for his gun. Kye launched himself forward and drove the knife straight into Dhal's chest. Beneath the force of the blow, Kye felt Dhal's ribs crack. His eyes went wild, and blood filled his mouth as he gaped at Kye, his mind unable to comprehend the trauma and pain. When Kye yanked the knife free from his sternum, Dhal collapsed to the floor.

Without waiting, Kye grabbed the handgun from Dhal's hip and, despite his hatred of the man, he fired two shots into his head to end his suffering. Kye was breathing hard, and he felt nausea overwhelm him as he looked from the brains splattered on the floor to where

Max lay. His once intimidating and massive form was crumpled on the floor in a pile of blood, the jagged glass still sticking out of his eye socket.

"Goodbye, old man," Kye said, swallowing the bile in his mouth. He turned from the room and closed the door behind him. When the lock clicked into place, Kye felt momentary relief. He was free from that room at least.

The cell he'd been in was at the end of the basement. Kye was quick to exit the hallway and wasn't entirely sure what to expect when he made his way upstairs. There was only one exit to the clubhouse and that was through the main room upstairs. Judging by the light streaming through the windows, it was nearing midday.

Kye made it three steps into the room when the first club member noticed him. The shocked gasp was the proverbial record scratch that drew the rest of the room's attention. Kye must have been a sight. Bruised, beaten, and covered in two men's blood, Kye had Max's knife in one hand and Dhal's pistol in the other.

"What do we do?" a prospect whispered as Kye slowly made his way through the room. The onlookers watched him as he moved with the singular focus of leaving. There was a mixture of awe and shock on their faces. Their titan and once leader turned abdicator had survived Max's torture room.

Kye stopped when he saw Riggs and Hamilton along

with two other men walking toward him. Lifting the pistol, Kye didn't hesitate to shoot Riggs straight between the eyes. The Wall Kats screamed in horror, and every armed man in the room drew their weapon. Hamilton had his gun aimed at Kye who lifted his hands in surrender.

"I was brought into this club by blood," Kye called loud enough to the room as he held his hands in the air, his shoulders still burning from captivity. "I've paid the blood price to leave." Silence overtook the room once more. Some members seemed torn between aiming their guns to shoot Kye or to defend him.

"You're leaving?" Hamilton asked as he stepped over Rigg's dead body as though it was no more than a door-mat. Kye nodded.

"Either in a body bag or on my feet, I'm not staying," Kye said, matter-of-factly. Hamilton considered him for a moment and glanced around the room.

"Kye Driscoll," he called loudly, "You've seen fit to withdraw your position in the Screaming Demons. As you came into this club by blood, I hereby accept your resignation and payment in blood. Brothers, let him leave."

The collective sound of guns uncocking was the only sound that could be heard. Kye's boots clicked loudly on the ground as he moved the rest of the way, pausing only briefly at Hamilton's side to surrender Max's knife.

Handing it to him hilt first, Kye met his eyes and clapped a hand on his shoulder. "Do better," he bid, and Hamilton nodded with the slight glare at Rigg's dead body.

The sun felt warm on Kye's face, and the breath of fresh air was a godsend. He saw his bike parked where he'd left it, and shuffled that way before he realized he didn't have the keys.

"You're going to need these." Kye turned and saw Jez standing behind him with the keys dangling from her fingers. She handed them over, and Kye held her hand firmly when he took them. "I didn't tell Max," Jez said, her watery eyes fixed on him. Kye searched her face for a moment and nodded once. He knew all too well what it was like to be caught in Max's web, but he also knew she was telling the truth. "I'm going to miss you, KD."

"Do yourself a favor, Jezebel," Kye said, straddling his bike. "Go find your son. He's your future."

"And Eliana is yours," Jez replied with a soft smile. Kye returned the gesture and kicked his bike to life. She placed a soft kiss on his cheek before stepping back and watching him ride away.

$\mathcal{E}$liana was sick of being in a vehicle. Currently stuck on the side of the road with a flat tire, with darkness rapidly approaching, Grier seemed just fine spending another night sleeping in the back of the SUV. Eliana, however, was ready to crawl out of her skin.

"Best to leave the flat on and change it in the morning," Grier said, pulling the long nail from the tire and tossing it into the brambles. They'd managed to make it to Oklahoma in the last day, and it seemed as though Grier was spending less time doubling back and more time driving. Silently.

"I can't take another night in the SUV," she said firmly.

"Sleep outside then," Grier said, opening the back and unrolling his sleeping bag.

"I'm not kidding. I'm going insane," she said, raking a hand through her hair. "Day in and out, we've been at this for four days."

"Feels more like five," Grier replied, but his tone was clearly sarcastic.

"Please just change the tire. We can find our way to a town and get a nice motel room with a real bed and a hot shower."

"I'll change it in the morning," Grier said, climbing inside and stretching out in the back. He crossed his legs and tucked his hands behind his head as though he was reclining on a king-size mattress in a five-star hotel suite. Eliana let out an angry growl and started fumbling with the toolbox.

"Forget it, I'll do it myself," she muttered and started pulling items out of the red box.

"Do you even know how to change a tire?" Grier asked without opening his eyes.

"I went to Harvard Law School, I think I can figure out how to change a tire," she threw back at him. "Now… where is the thing that props up the car?"

"The jack?"

"Yeah, the jack."

"We don't have one. Hence why I'm going to wait until morning. Figure I'll walk to town early before it gets hot and come back with a tow truck."

"Are you kidding me?" Eliana asked in exasperation.

"You've got like, five hundred guns back here and no jack?"

"I had a jack, but I had to take it out when we were back at the warehouse," Grier said, fishing a flask out of his pocket and downing a swig of alcohol.

"Why? Why would you do that?"

"Had to make room for my guns," he said with a cheeky smile.

"Don't you think a jack is more important that one more gun?"

"Not if I'm in a gunfight," he answered. "What if Max's men caught up to us? Can't throw a tire jack at them." Eliana let out another aggravated snarl and slammed the toolbox shut. "Giving up? I thought you were going to change the tire."

"I can't exactly change a tire without a car jack; maybe I could use one of your guns to prop the car up."

"Why don't you use your law degree to prop the car up?"

"Or maybe I'll just use your fat head," she suggested as she climbed into the back next to him and used her own sleeping bag as a pillow. Without responding, Grier passed her the flask, and she accepted it without a word. Staring at the ceiling of the car, Eliana shifted uncomfortably.

"You know what your problem is?" Grier asked in an uncharacteristic pursuit of conversation.

"Besides not having a car jack?"

"It's your attitude." Grier shifted so he could look at her. Though the back of the hummer was spacious, it felt cramped with their sleeping bags and his duffle of firearms.

"My attitude? What are you, my parent?" Even as she asked the question, she could hear the teenage level of maturity behind it.

"You see being out on the road as another form of captivity," he said observantly.

"Well, isn't it? You're not letting me leave, drive, or have any say in where we go or stay…"

"That's semantics," he said with a dismissive wave of his hand. "You have to think about it differently. What is a road?"

"Asphalt."

"Come on, seriously," Grier said in an almost pleading manner. He was laying on his side facing her, and the expression on his face was almost boyish. Sighing, Eliana rolled onto her side as well to mimic his posture. Propping her head on her upraised hand, she thought for a moment.

"A road is… what you use to get places. It's a path between destinations," she said with a slight shake of her head. Roads were one of those strange things she'd sort of taken for granted most of her life. Never having to really explain what they were because they'd always been around.

"See, that's what most people think," Grier responded, and he seemed almost excited at the prospect of explaining something different to her. "But that's what a member of the Screaming Demons, or really almost any motorcycle club, has figured out. The road isn't a means to an end. It's not just what you use to get places."

"What is it then?" Eliana asked, feeling a sense of curiosity overtake her. Despite her aggravation, she was at least momentarily and pleasantly distracted with some conversation.

"The road is the destination. When you decide that you're happy in the places in between, you're happy no matter where you go." Eliana let his words sink in for a moment. His reasoning had some wisdom to it.

Having spent most of her life perpetually dissatisfied with where she was, always striving to be somewhere else, the notion of being happy in the in-between was revolutionary. She made a soft humming noise that she understood what he meant and almost agreed with him.

"Is that how you and Kye feel when you're out on the road? Riding your motorcycles?" she asked, and Grier smiled.

"Yeah, I guess it is. Long rides aren't about getting from one place to the next; it's about enjoying the trip.

The longer the better. Nothing but open road and silence… it's a beautiful thing."

"How do you handle all that quiet, though? Nothing but your thoughts going around and around. I feel like I'm going insane," she admitted.

"That's part of your problem too," Grier said, still grinning. She hated the way he seemed to have her all figured out, even though they'd barely shared any information with each other. "You're the intellectual type."

"That's a bad thing?" she asked with her brows drawn together in confusion. Here she thought being smart was a good thing.

"You've got an academic mind," he said as though he were talking about gum on the bottom of a shoe. "You always have to put it to work. Thinking. Solving. Obsessing. You never let your mind just relax and turn off. Your thoughts always have to have a purpose or a problem to solve. You need to learn to just…" He trailed off and took an exaggerated inhale and exhale, "Breathe. Just learn to breathe and let your mind be quiet. You can find tranquility on the open road."

"Finding peace in the in-between?" she asked and decided she liked Grier's bohemian perspective on travel. Obviously, he was perfectly at ease driving for hours on end with nothing to occupy his thoughts or think obsessively over. In fact, now that she thought of it, when Grier was driving, nothing seemed to bother him at all. It was only when they were stopped and she was pestering him did he seem to get the least bit riled up.

"Exactly," he said, satisfied that he'd gotten his point across, and she'd understood. He lay fully on his back and tucked his arms behind his head once again. Eliana copied his posture.

Taking a deep breath, she tried to still her thoughts. Having only suffered through three yoga sessions in her life, she wasn't altogether unfamiliar with the concept of meditation, but it was hardly something she enjoyed let alone was any good at. When her first breath only reminded her they were stranded on the side of the road somewhere in Oklahoma, she tried another deep breath.

The second one brought back thoughts of how she'd felt like she was suffocating in the makeshift body bag Kye had put her in when they tried to fake her death and burial. She attempted a third deep breath which was much harder to take in because thoughts of Kye made her want to burst into tears. So, she attempted a fourth deep breath.

"Okay, now you're just going to make yourself pass out," Grier said, exasperated.

"Well, it's not working!" she complained, sitting up. "I can't just…" She inhaled sharply and exhaled in an almost cough "Turn all my thoughts off? I'm not wired that way! I like to think."

"No, you've convinced yourself you need to think; there's a difference," he said, and Eliana rolled her eyes. Grier turned his back to her and rummaged through the side compartment of the door for a moment. "Here," he said, handing her what he'd retrieved.

"What is this?" she asked, looking at the book he'd handed her. Grier was already laying back with his eyes closed again, this time his arm was draped over his eyes.

"Bought you a book at the last gas station," he replied curtly. Eliana flicked on the overhead light and saw it wasn't just a book, it was a 'Learn to Speak Spanish' book. "You'll need it when we get to Belize."

"Wow…" she said, strangely stricken by the sentiment. In school, she'd studied Latin as a prerequisite to her law degree. Though she knew some Spanish, it was mostly functional for ordering off the menu, not in a conversation. "Thank you."

"You're welcome," he said flatly. Eliana flipped through a few pages. Her mind was already racing with excitement. At this rate, she could master Spanish by the time they got there!

"Grier," she said after a moment. He let out a sigh. Clearly, he was hoping the book would give her something to do besides talk.

"Hmm?"

"Is 'Grier' your first name or your last name?" she asked. It had dawned on her during their previous conversation. He seemed to have her perfectly pegged, and she didn't know the first thing about him. It was unnerving.

"My name is Grier," he said after a brief hesitation.

"Grier," Eliana replied scrunching her face. "You don't look like a 'Grier'."

* * *

KYE HAD JUST FINISHED RAIDING his first warehouse when he was forced to stop for the night. His ribs ached terribly, and his eye was still swollen which made riding difficult. He'd managed to make it to the southern part of New Hampshire before fatigue overtook him.

The motel room he'd stopped at was cheap but clean. Thank God the water was hot too. As he stood under the shower, the steaming water hitting his back, he could see the water pooling at his feet was stained brownish red from the caked blood. More than just physical exhaustion, Kye felt emotionally drained. He'd killed Max, the closest thing he'd ever had to a father. Not that he'd been a great one, but he'd been the only one he'd ever known. At least, he assumed he was dead… a broken glass to the eyeball he was almost certain was a fatal wound.

Dhal he didn't give two shits about. Hell, that had been the icing on the cake. Killing Riggs, in hindsight probably wasn't a great idea. It would only contribute to the chaos the club would fall into. But he'd be damned if he was going to let the Demons pass to that raping bastard. Hamilton was old and would need to put the positions of rank to a vote by the patched members.

Kye slammed a fist on the wall of the shower. Reality sank in. He'd abdicated. Finally. Was he emotionally ready to do that? The club he'd spent the last decade being a part of was now behind him. Kye didn't know who he was without Max and the Demons. The old man had been right when he'd surmised that Kye had always had divided loyalties, but that was a life that Kye had gotten used to.

Spending so many years working toward something, now it was here, but he didn't feel ready for it. Logistically, sure. All his offshore accounts and warehouses were primed and ready. That wasn't the issue. Kye had assumed when the day came to leave, he'd do so on his own two feet and comfortable. This felt… messy. Ugly. But that was the way of things.

He'd been brought into the club by blood. Max had thrown the first punch the day he'd been beaten as initiation as prospect. Poetically, Max had dealt the final blow that had freed him too. In his own way, Kye had freed Max too. There was little chance he'd survive the wound to his face, especially given his condition. So it was Kye's blow that would free Max from this life.

The water from the shower ran over his face and diluted the salty tears that streamed down his cheeks. Kye stayed that way until the hot water ran cold, and he stepped out of the shower shivering, but much more relaxed. Surveying his reflection in the mirror, he saw why it had been so hard to see out of his right eye. One of the punches had broken open the skin just beneath his eyebrow, and it was full of fluid.

Using a sterile needle from his first aid kit, he punctured the blistered cut and let it drain before applying a topical ointment and bandage. His ribs were bruised badly, but binding them would make it impossible to ride the next day. Despite his exhaustion tempting him to spend the next week in bed, he was only giving himself this one night to hydrate, eat, and rest in a bed. After stopping at his warehouse, he saw that he was four days behind Grier and Eliana. He'd tried calling one of Grier's burner phones, but it went straight to voicemail. Not that it would do any good. He wouldn't delay them even if he did get ahold of them.

The sooner Eliana was out of the country and at the safe house in Belize, the better. Grier was reliably covering their tracks, taking the long way to get there. If there was a hit still in place on Eliana, he'd need the diversion to keep them concealed. If Kye's strength held out, he might be able to catch up to them before they crossed the border. If not, then he'd just have to catch up with her on the beach. Either way, he was free, and in a few days' time, he was going to have Eliana in his arms.

He didn't know who he was without the Demons, but he was pretty sure, whoever it was, belonged with Eliana.

8

Eliana was in heaven. Not literal heaven, but in her mind, this was the closest thing to it. Which, at the moment, was a single occupant bathtub in the motel bathroom. After their last night on the side of the road, she had accompanied Grier on his walk into town. Though they'd risen early, the Oklahoma heat in summer was humid and dry. Not to mention the fact that the nearest town to where they'd been stranded was almost ten miles from the car. At first, she'd been excited at the prospect of walking instead of driving, but by the fourth mile, she was longing for air conditioning. When the sun had crested the horizon, it brought with it sweltering heat that turned the pavement into a proverbial baking sheet in the oven.

When they'd finally reached town, it was another two hours before they could secure a tow truck to take them back to swap out the tire. Then getting back to town was another hour altogether. By then, even Road Zen Grier was in a salty mood and ready for reprieve. It hadn't taken much persuading on her part for them to take a detour through the local motel. They booked two adjoining rooms for the night, and the first thing Eliana had done was lock the door, strip down, and nearly drown herself in a cold shower to cool down.

Using the entire novelty size bottle of motel shampoo she'd been provided, she scrubbed the five-day-old grease out of her hair and had used the entire bar of soap to wash her body and shave. She hadn't realized how gross she felt until she'd scraped off the layer of grime she'd been sporting. The motel offered an on-sight laundromat for the long-term tenants, but they accepted quarters. She'd tossed in a load of laundry, even feeling generous enough to wash a few of Grier's things, in exchange for him going to town and buying them a real meal.

"If it's served in a paper sack with little packets of ketchup I'm going to murder you," she'd yelled at Grier as he left. He'd waved a hand back at her and driven off, though not without several warnings that if she left the motel room for any reason other than to switch the laundry he was going to intentionally drag out their trip another week. She didn't want to risk that threat. So here she sat in a bathtub of warm water, feet propped on the edge, reading her book of Spanish phrases and vocabulary, happy to be anywhere but in that damned car.

When the water turned too cold for her to bear, she stood and wrapped herself in a large towel and shuffled into the room. The air-conditioned unit in the window was on full blast and, with the curtains drawn, she dropped the towel and let the icy air blow over her skin. Compared to the near heat stroke she'd suffered that morning, this was pure bliss. Dressing in shorts and a t-shirt, she slipped on the only pair of flats she'd brought and scuffled down to the laundry room.

There was a woman sitting in the corner reading a magazine with headphones in, but otherwise, the room was unoccupied. Eliana didn't have a basket, so she was forced to carry their clothes in her arms on her way back up to their rooms. The TV was on and playing afternoon news stories while she folded the clothes. When she'd stacked Grier's clothes in a neat pile, she decided to drop them off in his room.

He'd insisted that they keep the doors between their rooms unlocked so it was easy to cross over. She noted that he'd brought in the duffle bag of guns and left it sitting on the edge of the bed. "Jeez," she breathed when she saw how many there were. Even though she knew he'd brought them for protection, having so many guns around didn't make her feel any safer.

She still remembered what it had felt like holding that gun to her temple. Not knowing at the time it wasn't loaded, it had been the real deal in her mind when she'd pulled that trigger. The clicking sound still haunted her. Eliana never wanted to know what it was like to be on the receiving end of the barrel of a gun ever again. Holding one of the weapons in her hand, it felt heavier than the gun she'd held before. Assuming that meant it was loaded, she set it back down.

In the side pockets of the duffle were four blank passports, a massive envelope of hundred-dollar bills, and a second one full to the brim of several types of foreign currency. Zipping the side back up, Eliana looked one more time in the main compartment. That's when she saw it.

Tossed haphazardly in the bag was Grier's cell phone. As if seeing some strange anomaly, she picked it up the way you might hold a large wad of cash you just happened upon in the street. Before she knew what she was doing, Eliana was turning it on and watching the screen light up. Her breathing had stopped as she held it, and when the single message of 'one missed call' came up, she shuddered and hit the voicemail icon.

"On my way."

A sob burst suddenly out of her. It was Kye! It had been Kye's voice. Her fingers forgot how to function as she desperately tried to figure out how to check the time when the call had come in. Finally figuring it out, the unmarked number registered that it had come in the day before. Her elation blinded her temporarily, but as she thought longer on it, she wondered why Grier hadn't checked his phone. Why didn't he have it on him now? Had he given up hope that Kye was alive? Then what was the point of leaving the country? Was he really so committed to escaping from anywhere Max might find them that he was going to leave the country with her? He didn't even like her!

Eliana tried to dial the number back, but the automated message that the number she was trying to reach had already been disconnected deflated any bubbling hope that she might be able to speak with him. It wasn't enough to completely dampen her mood, though. Kye was alive, and he was coming to meet them. Now it didn't matter where they were headed or how long it took to get there, he was on his way, and soon they'd be together!

"WHERE IS IT?" Grier snapped as the door between their rooms slammed open. Eliana was lounging on her motel bed watching TV and hadn't realized he was back until just this moment. He carried take-out in one hand and a grocery sack in the other, but the furious look on his face was what caught her attention.

"Where is what?" she asked, feigning ignorance.

"You know what!"

"I do?"

"I swear to God, Eliana, you might be my best friend's girl, but I will shoot you in the face. Where is the cell phone?"

"Oh, this?" she asked, pulling it from under the pillow next to her. Grier lunged forward, but she held it at bay. "Before I give it back, you need to tell me why you didn't have it on you and why it hasn't been turned on this whole time!" He looked startled for a moment. "Yeah that's right, I figured it out, Road Boy," she taunted. "You kept it plugged into the console so I'd think you were monitoring it, but you weren't. The phone hasn't even been turned on! That's why you never checked it, and that's why it didn't ring when Kye called yesterday!"

"What?" he asked, and the bags fell out of his hands. "Give it to me."

"No!" she protested, but he grabbed it out of her hand anyway. He scrolled through the phone and saw there was a saved message. She allowed him a moment to listen to the message before smiling in satisfaction. "See? An intellectual mind isn't always a bad thing."

"It's not always a good thing, you idiot," he said,

pocketing the device. "You know why I didn't turn it on? Because we're not at the meeting spot yet!"

"Huh?"

"God," he breathed and pinched the bridge of his nose. "Kye and I use synced burner phones. When I turn mine on it pings to his letting him know I've turned it on."

"So?"

"So, I'm not supposed to turn it on until we're at the Luxury Motel in El Paso. I rent room 44 and turn the phone on. He knows that I'm in the motel waiting for him with clean passports and ready to cross the border. He was supposed to arrive the next day, with you might I add, and the three of us would cross together. Obviously, things got a little reversed, but now he's going to think that we're there instead of here!"

"What's the big deal, we just get in the car and drive to El Paso. We can be there in, what? Fifteen hours? That's cake compared to how long we've been driving!" Eliana defended and swung her legs over the side of the bed to stand.

"You'd think it would be that easy," Grier said, stooping to pick up the fallen containers of take-out food and setting them on the small, round table across the room.

"Why isn't it?"

"Because this damned heatwave we're experiencing

burnt out the radiator in the Hummer!" he practically shouted. "I managed to get it back to the auto shop we got the tow truck from, but it's going to be at least a two-day repair. We're stuck here."

"Can't we get another car?"

"You want to put a rental car on your credit card and have Max meet us there?" he asked sarcastically.

"Okay… what if we buy one? Nothing fancy, just an old, beat-up clunker. I saw that stash of money in your room. We can buy something for a couple of grand."

"Sweetheart," he said in a patronizing way that irked her, "if my brand-new Hummer couldn't survive driving in this heatwave across town to pick up your stupid organic groceries, then how in the hell are we going to get a clunker across the state and part of Texas?" It was a valid question, but Eliana didn't like it for the sheer fact that she had no way of answering it.

"Okay, so… so we're just a little late meeting Kye in El Paso. That's no big deal. We'll get the car fixed and be a little late. He'll wait for us," she said, more to convince herself than anything.

"Yeah, and every day he lingers in the same location is a day closer to death. If Kye got out then that can mean only one thing— he's being chased and by a lot of men. No way in hell would Max let him go without sending everyone after him."

"All of this could have been avoided if you'd just told

me from the start what the plan was," Eliana barked, feeling suddenly defensive.

"Oh, because you have a history of sticking to plans once you've been informed of the details." She didn't know what she hated more, his sarcasm, his condescension, or his eye-roll. "Here," he said, dumping the grocery bag on her bed. "Eat your fucking kale."

* * *

KYE PULLED his bike to a standstill at the gas station pump off the main freeway. He felt good about how many miles he'd made it and counted his blessing that so far he'd managed to hit the open road. When the nozzle of the hose was resting in the open cap and gas flowed freely, he pulled the phone from his pocket.

There were no text messages or missed calls, and though he was hoping for one, he didn't expect it. Grier was much more disciplined in following protocol than he was. Had the roles been reversed, he wouldn't have been able to keep himself from contacting Eli. Every muscle in his body ached for her. Even more than it ached from the bruises he brandished.

Every delay felt like agony knowing he was playing catch up in all of this. He wanted to make sure he met them before they crossed the border. If Grier had already secured them passports, it would take longer for

Kye to meet them. He didn't have the supplies he needed nor did he have Grier's expedited efficiency. Even though his break from the club was supposed to be clean, having paid the exit price, he still didn't trust it. The memories of torture, beatings, and murder attempts were still too fresh.

Once they'd had some downtime in Belize, maybe a few months of staying low and off the radar, they could cross back into the country under their real names and identities. This would eventually allow them to work if that's what they decided. Kye's nest egg of well over a million dollars was enough to sustain them, likely, for the rest of their lives. But he also knew his woman. Eliana wasn't the type to spend the rest of her life lying around.

Although, if Kye had any say, they'd spend their first week in Belize fucking each other on every surface he could find. It was insatiable how much he craved her. Having never taken drugs, he could only imagine this was the way a junkie jonesed for a fix. He needed her. So, when he saw the alert on his mobile map app, he fumbled to open it. Grier had turned on the ping alert. This was his signal that he'd arrived at the border destination of El Paso.

"Damn," Kye muttered to himself as he removed the gas nozzle. They were two days ahead of schedule. The plan was for them to spend at least seven days on the road making sure they weren't being tailed then make their way there. Something must have happened to accelerate the timeline. Maybe someone had found them, or they'd been robbed and lost the ten grand in cash Kye had stashed for them in the marked warehouse in Kentucky.

Kye paid for the gas and mounted before turning on the GPS tracker. He'd have to ride all night to catch them. He was only just outside of Indianapolis, Indiana. It was at least another twenty hours to El Paso and that was only if his bike and his body didn't give out. He didn't have a choice. The bike roared to life, headlights flicked on, and Kye was once again racing along Highway 44 in desperation to get to Eliana.

$\mathcal{E}$liana had finished her third shower in two days and was styling her hair in the mirror. It had been too long since she'd put on any makeup or a styled outfit, and she was starting to feel it. While never one for flawless manicures and high heels, she still liked having that element of being dressed nicely on occasion. So, after two days cooped up in the motel in Oklahoma, she'd decided she and Grier needed to go out to dinner.

"Why?" he asked as he sat watching a racing show on the TV in his room. He was eating stale French fries out of the bag and staring mindlessly as the racing bikes made dangerous and high-speed turns.

"Because, if you don't, I'm going to pick up this phone," she began and held up the phone on the nightstand by his bed, "and tell the police you kidnapped me.

I'll tell them you're armed, dangerous, and they should shoot to kill."

"I'd rather you didn't," he said, still not looking at her.

"Grier!" she pleaded. "You haven't let me out of the motel room since our first night. This is almost worse than the car. Please, can we just go into town and have dinner at a real restaurant, grab a beer, and then we can come right back."

"The car will be ready in the morning. We'll have dinner in El Paso with Kye," he said flippantly. Eliana gritted her teeth and picked the phone up again.

"Hello?" she said into the receiver. "Is this the front desk?" Grier glanced at her out of the corner of his eye. "Yes, can you connect me with the local police depar…" Her words were cut off as Grier leaped across the room, over the bed, and tackled her. "Grier!" she screamed as he straddled her and slammed the phone down. "Get off me," she groaned and wiggled underneath him.

"Don't do that," he said with a warning finger in her face. He stood and didn't so much as extend a hand to help her up. "Fine, we'll go to dinner," he consented. Grabbing his wallet from the nightstand, he groaned when he saw the expectant look on her face. "Now what?"

"Let's have a nice dinner," she suggested. "I'm going to go get cleaned up, why don't you do the same?"

"I look fine," he protested. Eliana crossed her arms. Okay, so his pants were covered in French fry grease, he hadn't showered yet, and his t-shirt was for some obscure 80s band no one had ever heard of. "I'm not going to win this argument, am I?"

"Probably not," she admitted.

"I hate you," he grumbled and before she could even take a step, he had pulled his shirt off and was going for his belt buckle.

"Wait!" she screeched, holding a hand over her eyes. "At least wait for me to be out of the room!"

"So, hurry up and go!" he yelled back, clearly not the least bit phased by her modesty. Eliana closed the door to their adjoining rooms behind her, trying to squelch the blush on her face.

As much as she couldn't stand Grier most of the time, mainly because their confinement put them in non-stop proximity of each other, and Eliana suspected he was the type who needed as much alone time as she did, there was no denying he was an attractive man.

He was tall, almost painfully by the way she usually needed to crane her neck to see him, and definitely taller than Kye. His skin was permanently tan just based on his complexion and his shorter curly hair was always slicked back into nice waves. Although she'd spent more time on the wrong end of a glare than she appreciated, she had to admit, he had the most incredible green eyes. There were times when they were dark like the ocean and then others, most often when he was driving and staring off into the horizon, that they were a pale and ethereal green.

So when he entered her room via the adjoining door dressed in a white v-neck, dark denim jeans, and boots, she felt the blush creep over her face. Though she'd tried to cover her eyes quickly, she'd still gotten an excellent view of his toned chest and torso when he'd ripped his dirty shirt off.

"You look nice," she complimented and went back to applying her makeup.

"Thanks," he replied and flopped on her bed, legs crossed in that easy manner while he waited for her. A minute later Eliana stepped out of the bathroom in a pink maxi dress and flip flops. Her hair was curled and she wore her nicest necklace. "Great, let's go," he said, standing.

"Wait," she beckoned, "aren't you going to tell me I look nice too?" She firmly planted her hands on hips. His eyes shifted as though she'd asked some ridiculous question like 'how many licks does it take to get to the center of the moon?'

"Hadn't planned on it, no," he replied sincerely.

"What a gentleman," she said sarcastically and grabbed her purse. Grier made an exaggerated display of opening the door and bowed low as he gestured for her to leave first.

"My lady," he said in a drooling voice. Eliana rolled her eyes this time and stepped outside. She waited for him to lock their doors before they made their way into town.

Though it was still blisteringly hot considering it was nearly dark, there was a nice steakhouse not too far from the motel that they decided to dine at. The decor was dated, but the food was amazing. Grier opted for the porterhouse and Eliana got the New York strip, and they each had a glass of wine and a side of baked potatoes.

"See?" Eliana asked when they'd settled the bill and were heading back outside, "that wasn't so bad, was it?" Her knowing look made Grier chuckle.

"No, it wasn't," he replied and turned to head back to the motel.

"Uh-uh," she said, grabbing his arm. "You paid for dinner, I'm buying drinks," she said, dragging him the opposite direction.

"That wasn't part of the deal," he complained as she forced him to fall in step with her.

"Come on, there is a bar and pool hall just down the road. I can hear the music from the patio. Let me kick your ass in pool a couple of times, and I'll pay for your drinks," she offered. Though he looked displeased at first, at the mention of drinks he seemed to brighten.

"You're crazy if you think you're going to beat me in pool," he goaded, and Eliana smiled as she linked her arm through his.

"Since I'm going to get you fairly soused tonight, I think it's possible," she responded with a laugh.

"I don't think you brought enough cash with you to get me drunk," he stated as they finally reached the bar. Sure enough, a loud but not very talented band was playing watered down karaoke music on the patio, and just inside there were four pool tables, three of which were not currently being used.

Grier went to get quarters while Eliana bought a pitcher of beer and brought over two glasses. "You have to break," she said, pouring the amber liquid into their cups and starting in on hers.

"What are we betting?" he asked as he racked the balls.

"Cash is too boring," she said, playing along with his game. "How about, a fact for every ball. You sink one I'll answer a question, I sink one you have to answer a question?"

"What if I don't want to ask you any questions," he said dryly, and Eliana dropped her chin and narrowed her eyes.

"Fine, how about every ball is ten minutes I have to be quiet on the road tomorrow?" she offered.

"Done, and you have to take a drink," he said, pointing.

"Deal," she agreed. It had been many years since she drank to the point of getting drunk, but she wasn't going to waste the night of Grier's good mood on being prudish. Grier lifted the triangle and brandished his pool cue. With a hard crack, he broke, and immediately two striped balls dropped into pockets.

"Drink!" he ordered, and Eliana sighed. Taking two large swigs, she eyed the half-empty pitcher.

"My turn," she said, hopping up. Always being a geometry whiz, pool wasn't too hard to master and on her first try, she sank a solid in the side pocket.

"Fuck," Grier muttered.

"Okay," she said, turning to him, "you seem like a relatively decent guy... how come you don't have a girl of your own?"

"Easy," he said after downing a mouthful of his own drink, "don't want one." Eliana wasn't satisfied with the answer, but she accepted it. Her second shot missed, and when Grier was up, he sank another ball.

Sighing, she swigged the last of her beer and had to pour another one. The pitcher was already almost empty. They were going to need more beer.

* * *

"Shh," Eliana giggled as they stumbled back to the hotel. Damned him for booking rooms on the second floor! Grier's arm was dangling over her shoulders, and they both struggled up the steps and into the hallway. "Shh!" she said harshly again. About ten minutes before closing time, Grier had decided he could sing better than the guy in the band and hadn't stopped singing the entire way back. "Give me the key," she said, holding out her hand.

"I got it," he slurred and dug around in his pocket before fishing it out. He went to put the key in the lock, but missed and ended up punching the wall instead.

"Give it here," Eliana said, laughing. She moved Grier so he was leaning against the wall instead of her and unlocked the door. Stepping inside first, Grier was right behind her. He draped himself over her back, and she nearly collapsed under his weight.

"The room is spinning," he groaned with his cheek pressed to her shoulder. Eliana grunted as she turned and pushed him onto the bed. "That's better," he sighed, closing his eyes.

"You're so drunk," Eliana laughed as she helped him out of his boots. "God you've got massive feet," she noted and tossed his size thirteen boot into the corner.

"You know what they say about big feet," he chided with a grin.

"Yeah," she said, looking down at him, "they smell!" Grier chuckled and grabbed her arm and yanked her down on the bed beside him. "What are you doing?" she asked, feeling flushed when he rested his head on her chest.

"You're soft," he murmured and nuzzled against her. "You remember what I said before?" he asked vaguely. "About not wanting a girl?"

"Yeah..." she replied, suddenly very worried he'd gotten the wrong impression about their evening and was expecting more from her.

"It's true... never wanted a girl following me around everywhere, at least not girls like the ones at the club," he said and yawned. "But if I found a girl who was more like you... I could be okay with that." Eliana felt sincerely touched by his words. Grier wasn't the type to bestow a compliment on anyone, especially if he didn't like them.

The answer to her question if he was expecting more was answered when he rolled away from her, resting his head on his pillow instead, and in moments he was snoring. She chuckled. They weren't all that different. She'd needed to get out of the hotel, put on a dress and some makeup to feel human again, and maybe Grier had needed just a brief moment of human contact to feel the same.

She stood on unsteady legs, the room spinning for her as well, and made toward her room. Knowing she'd need water, she left Grier's room into the hall and filled a bucket of ice before walking back to her room. Even in her inebriated state, she thought it was off that her motel room door was unlocked. She distinctly remembered Grier locking it before they left.

Not daring to go into the room by herself, she slid back into Grier's room and began shaking his shoulder. "Grier, Grier, wake up! My door is unlocked, and I think someone is inside!" she whispered harshly. He was dead to the world, however. Didn't as much as flinch when she shook him as hard as she dared. "Fuck," she cursed and set the ice bucket down.

His duffle bag was still on the floor, so she decided it was better to arm herself with a gun than a motel ice bucket. Grabbing the easiest handgun, she cocked it and slowly slinked to the door between their rooms. Every noise she made seemed like the roar of a semi-truck. The handle wobbled, the door creaked, and the floorboards shifted underfoot.

When she managed to get the door open, she stepped inside the dark room and aimed the gun at anything and everything. Nothing seemed out of place and nothing moved. That is until the pillow on her bed shifted. Gasping, Eliana realized it wasn't a pillow but a person. Someone was in her room!

Debating whether she should shoot, run, or call the police, she stood there for much longer than reason would have dictated was safe considering there was an intruder. Needing to make any decision, she stepped forward and reached for the bedside lamp. Her hands were trembling as she fumbled with the switch until the light turned on.

"Too bright…" the figure on her bed muttered. Eliana gasped, much louder this time and aimed the gun directly at the person and fired. The empty gun clicked. "What the fuck!" she barely had time to register the yell when the gun in her hand was sent flying across the room. Staring up at her in panic was the most perfect set of blue eyes.

"Kye?" she breathed. His face was brandishing a few bruises and there was a bandaged cut under his left eyebrow, but it was definitely him. Flinging herself onto him, she buried her face in his neck and wept. "Kye, you're here, oh my God"

"Yeah, I'm here," he said in a tight voice. Holding her at arms-length she could see pain run across his face. "If you're so happy to see me, why did you try and shoot me?"

10

There were only a few times Grier had been able to admit he'd had too much to drink. This was one of them. Maybe it was the handful of long days on the road, poor hydration, lack of sleep and stress, but the beers from the night before had gotten to him. He could feel his headache before he was fully awake. The throbbing pain pulsed behind his eyes, and he was desperate for water.

Rolling out of bed, groaning in pain as every joint in his body hurt, he made his way to the bathroom for a glass of water. The lukewarm tap water from the bathroom tasted gross, but it helped quell his headache. The throbbing in his ears subsided enough that he could hear more than the pounding of his own heartbeat.

Too much.

The paper-thin walls did nothing to spare him the moaning from the room next door. That was exactly what he didn't need. By the sounds of it, they were really going at it. He didn't know whether it annoyed him that two people were having sex at nine in the morning while he had a hangover or the fact that he wasn't having sex at nine in the morning when he had a hangover.

Stepping back into the bedroom, he moved toward the wall opposite the adjoining door, but the moaning grew quieter. His eyes narrowed at the door. The sex noises couldn't possibly be coming from Eliana's room. Could they? Crossing the room in two long strides, the increase in volume confirmed his suspicions. Grier paled. There could only be three options as to what was happening, and they all required the gun he was pulling from his duffle bag.

The first, some guy from the bar last night had followed them back and was raping Eliana. In which case, Grier would shoot him. The second, Eliana had invited some guy from the bar back to the room, and they were having consensual sex in which case, he would shoot Eliana for cheating on his best friend. The third, Eliana had taken off leaving her room vacant and two strangers were having sex in the room to which Grier would shoot both of them for waking him up and making his head hurt worse.

Slamming the door between their rooms open, gun aimed, blood rushed to his face as he met a full view of Eliana's bare chest bouncing as she straddled someone underneath her.

"What the fuck?" he cried finger twitching on the trigger. So, she was fucking some guy!

"Grier!" Eliana screamed and clutched her hands over her chest.

"Grier!" The distinct barking anger of Kye resounded through the room. Hands still clutching her hips, Kye sat up and pulled Eliana flush against him to shield her bare torso from his eyes.

"Oh... hey, Kye," Grier said, uncocking his gun. "You caught up fast," he noted with his weapon lowered.

"Yeah, I did," Kye agreed with a look of bewilderment. Grier stood there for another moment almost expecting Kye to break out into a full explanation of who, what, where, when and how of everything when Eliana practically screamed at him.

"Get out!"

"Right, sorry!" Grier said, face beet red, and ducked out of the room, locking it behind him. With all the blood rushing to his face, his headache was decidedly worse. At this point, only the hair of the dog was going to cure anything, so he tucked his gun under his shirt and set off on foot for the bar they'd been at the night before. Shit, it wasn't like Kye and Eliana were going to emerge anytime soon.

* * *

"FUCK, DON'T STOP," Eliana moaned. After the door had closed, it hadn't taken them long to get back to their previous task, and Kye, though miserably sore from his bruised ribs, was managing to buck his hips under her so deliciously, she felt her toes curl.

His fingers were digging into her hip bones, rocking her back and forth as he pushed himself upward and inside her. God, she felt good. He loved the way her stomach contracted with each thrust, her soft skin glistening with sweat. Her breasts bounced the harder he drove into her, and he couldn't help but bury his face between the fleshy mounds. Eliana's fragrance was sweeter than he remembered. Skin tasking of honey, he kissed the silky skin of her areola before taking a nipple in his mouth.

Her persistent thrusts turned frenzied as she rocked herself into a climax. Biting his lip, he watched her face, flushed and rosy, her eyes squeezed closed and lips parted as she shook and trembled until she collapsed against him. As she shuddered, he took his satisfaction, and when he peaked, his ribs couldn't take anymore, and he collapsed onto his back.

"Are you in pain?" Eliana said, voice full of concern as she rolled onto her side and held a hand to his face. He grinned to cover his wince and turned to kiss her palm.

"I'm perfect," he said, looking at her. His blue eyes were full of mirth, but she could see the pain that lingered. His abdomen was covered in bruises that were a deep purple. The cut above his eye had been tended to, but it was still red and slightly swollen. She propped herself up on her elbow and leaned over to kiss it softly.

"You are perfect," she echoed and kissed him on the lips. He was warm, and his hand trailed up her side. Eliana melted into him, and she sighed.

"Tell me," she beckoned, eyes still closed. She'd asked him outright the night before what had happened. He'd distracted her with hot kisses and wandering hands. Not that she was complaining, but his stamina was spent and in truth, so was hers. Now as they lie on their sides facing one another, she needed him to comfort her with more than just his body. She needed his words to put her mind at ease.

He hurried through his explanation of how Max had been on to them from the start, but his removal of the empty body bag from the fake grave and discovery of the ranger's body in the garage had solidified it. Eliana was kicking herself for ever letting Kye stay. She should have known, no matter how hard they had tried, their plan was faulty at best.

"You're skipping details," Eliana noticed when Kye was intentionally vague about his treatment in the cells of the clubhouse.

"I am," confirmed Kye. He was still lying on his side and lightly running a hand down Eliana's spine as she lay on her stomach, her bare back warm to the touch.

"I want to know, Kye… I need to know," she said quietly, her eyes focused on the pillow in front of her.

"You don't need to know," he argued. Her stern eyes turned on him.

"That's not for you to decide," she protested. "If it hadn't been for me, this wouldn't have happened."

"Yes, it would have," Kye contradicted. "Max was determined. He'd caught me in his web, and whether it was you or something else, the outcome would have been the same."

"I don't agree," Eliana said, rolling out of bed. Kye reached for her, but she was already moving toward her suitcase where she pulled on a long t-shirt. As she pulled on a pair of white panties, Kye managed to sit up in bed. Her hands moved to her hips as she stared down at him.

"It's not that bad…"

"Kye," she said seriously, "you're covered in bruises, your nose looks like it's been broken recently, and I could feel the welts on your back when you were…"

"When I was what? Fucking you?" he asked with a coy smile. Her eyes narrowed.

"You're not going to distract me. I want to know, and you need to tell me," she demanded. "What did Max do to you?"

"Max did relatively little," Kye said and chuckled when she crossed her arms in anger. Her nipples were still taut under her shirt and they, like her eyes, had fixed him with a pointed stare. "He ordered Dhal to do most of the dirty work."

"Bastard," Eliana huffed out. Kye held out his arms to her, and she crawled over the bed to him. He hoisted her over his lap so she was straddling him again. From this vantage point, he could hold her gaze indefinitely without her looking away. "He was the one who did this?" she asked, trailing her thumb over the cut under his eyebrow.

"Yes," Kye answered. She leaned forward and placed a delicate kiss on the bandage.

"And this?" she asked, running her hands down his chest where she could see small but angry-looking cigar burns and fist-sized bruises.

"Mmmhmm," Kye murmured. He could feel himself growing hard again, and when she peppered kisses over his pectorals and toward his abs, he fisted a handful of her hair, drawing her mouth back to his in a burning kiss.

"This happened because of me," she said, pressing her forehead against his.

"This happened because of Max. Because he needed to have control over me. Max couldn't stand the idea that my loyalty was divided between him and you. He was wrong from the start. My loyalty was never divided."

"What do you mean?"

"It was you. It's always been you, Eli," he said sincerely, cupping her face with both hands. "I got lost for a while… trying to have everything. In the end, everything was for you. I want this life together. You and me."

"In Belize?" she asked with a small smile.

"On the fucking moon if it means we're together," he laughed, and she kissed him firmly on the mouth. Taking her by the waist, he jerked her forward so his erection nestled snuggly between her legs. Her moan moved through him, and his tongue pushed inside her mouth to taste her.

"Kye," she breathed when he moved to kiss her neck just under her ear. "Don't ever send me away again."

"I promise," he whispered in her ear.

"Promise?"

"Yes, I swear it."

"Good," she said, sliding a hand between them to grab hold of his cock. He hissed a sharp intake of breath when she squeezed him. "Because if you do, I will hunt you down, and I will cut this off." He would have assumed she was teasing, but her powerful hold and the ferocity in her eyes led him to believe otherwise. She was entirely serious.

"Cut it off, burn it, and scatter the ashes," he said, involuntarily grinding against her hand, "it's all yours anyway."

"You want me to cut it off?" she asked bemused.

"Not particularly," he answered, "it has… other uses."

"Like what?" The way she was looking at him with rounded eyes, her bottom lip tucked between her teeth, he lost all thought. Without moving her an inch from his lap, he tore the thin fabric of her panties from her body, and she squealed when he flipped her onto her back.

The heat between their bodies was palpable. Like two magnets, they fused together effortlessly, and when Kye sheathed himself inside her, her soft and wet warmth enveloping him, they moaned simultaneously. Unlike the night before and again that morning, Kye took the dominant position. Despite his aching ribs, the ache in his cock was more urgent.

Eliana's hands crawled over his back, the knotted welts still prominent on his skin. She'd done her best to be gentle in her touches, delicate and aware of his wounds, but the way he drove into her, she was unable to refrain from clawing at his back. Kye groaned, the mixture of pain and pleasure sending his senses into overdrive.

"God, you feel good," he growled, sliding in and out of her. Eliana wrapped her legs around his waist and buried her face in his neck. The sheer size of him, strong and towering over her, was a heady and erotic feeling. Though his waist was trim and narrowed, the perfect width for her legs to wrap around, his chest was broad and his powerful thighs, thick from gripping his bike, were strong enough to drive into her relentlessly.

She knew he was holding back. The potential energy that pulsed beneath his skin like ripples on the water. Their first few times together, she could feel it too. His restraint, being gentle with her as her body adjusted. It made her love him even more. Now, perhaps it was because of the limitations his injuries were putting on him, but now she found his withholding almost an insult.

"I'm not going to break," she said in his ear when she could feel his pace slowing. "Stop holding back."

"You may not break, but I will," he said with gritted teeth.

"We can stop…"

"No," Kye chuckled, "we can't." Digging his hips into hers, she gasped and contracted around him. Using her hands to prop up his shoulders, the angle in which he pushed inside her was long and drawn out with each thrust. The muscles in her abs tightened as she rose up to meet him. Kye took both of her wrists and pinned her hands to the bed next to her head.

His lips crashed onto hers as he pressed her firmly into the mattress. The movement of his thrusts slowed considerably, and he drew himself out of her almost completely before sliding back inside. Her moan was throaty and deep and matched his perfectly. Their slow lovemaking burned like embers.

He released one of her hands and slid his between their bodies to press a thumb against her pearl. Without moving a muscle in response, she savored the intense feeling of his firm touch. Combined with his steady withdrawals and penetrations, her body thrummed with pleasure. Kye buried himself inside her, face pressed into her hair, sweat beading on his back, and legs bent between her. Rolling her hips in perfect rhythm with his, their torsos pressed together and tongues intertwining, Kye reached his peak first.

She held him tightly against her as he trembled and shuddered over the edge. He groaned her name while she clenched her walls around him, and moments later Eliana felt herself seizing in ecstasy. He remained inside her until he went soft, and her hands trailed up and down his spine. His breathing became steadier, and his body went limp.

"Kye," she whispered, and he made a humming noise

deep inside. Laughing softly, she gently rolled him off and out of her. He lay stretched on his back, fast asleep. Eliana smiled and pressed a gentle kiss to his forehead before tucking the covers around him, resting her head on his shoulder, and joining him in a blissful and contented slumber.

11

"Why did you change rooms?" Eliana asked. Grier was lounging in the driver's seat of the large vehicle, feet propped in the open window, sunglasses over his eyes. He pulled them lower on the bridge of his nose to stare at her. "I knocked on your door this morning only to find the room was now rented to a very grumpy Asian man." She opened the door behind him and tossed her bag into the back.

"As much fun as it was listening to you and Kye have an excessive amount of noisy sex the last two days, I chose a quieter room. One that was on the other side of the motel. I could still hear you."

"You could not," Eliana argued as she slammed the door.

"Excessive is a relative term," Kye chimed in as he

approached the vehicle from the other side. "Personally, I could have done with a little more." He tossed Eliana a wink, and she smiled.

"Can you two not? I don't want to have to clean up vomit off the steering wheel."

"Poor baby," Eliana teased and reached through the window to pinch his cheek.

"Fuck, can we go already?" Grier cried as he slapped her hand away. She laughed before rounding to the other side of the vehicle where Kye was. He opened the passenger door for her, and she crossed her arms.

"Uh-uh," Eliana said and pushed the door closed.

"We really need to get on the road," Kye said. "Three days in one place is too long. If there are any of the Demons looking for retribution…"

"Oh I know," she interrupted, "I'm riding with you," she declared and turned to look at Kye's Harley parked in the space next to them.

"You are?" he asked and matched her crossed arms. "It's a long drive to the next stop."

"I know."

"I think you'd be more comfortable in the Hummer."

"I've been cooped up in that damn vehicle way too long," she stated, stepping closer to him, chin tilted upward at a sharp angle to meet his eyes. "I'm riding with you. It's almost ten hours to El Paso, and I am not going to go that long without my arms wrapped around you." Kye smiled as she did just that, arms encircling his waist. Pulling her up onto her tiptoes, he kissed her, both hands tangling in her hair.

"Kill me now," Grier complained and made an exaggerated gagging noise. Kye flipped him off, lips still planted firmly on Eliana's, but they parted when she couldn't help but laugh.

"Poor Grier," she taunted, head leaned against Kye's shoulder.

"I'll live, now can we go? Please?"

"Grab a helmet," he instructed, and Eliana kissed his cheek before moving over to the Harley. Kye made his way around to Grier's open window and leaned against the frame where his friend's feet had just been. "I know we haven't had much time to talk these last couple of days," Kye said in a slightly apologetic tone.

"You were busy," Grier said flatly. "Besides, I think I can piece a few things together. Scars speak for themselves," he stated, indicating the now permanent scar above Kye's eye just under his eyebrow.

"I appreciate you not asking, but that doesn't mean you don't deserve an explanation," Kye replied.

"I never needed one, Kye. Max was going to impose his agenda regardless. If you had gone down, I still would have left. Still would have skipped town and gone ahead with our exit strategy."

"With Eli?"

"If you hadn't have been around to protect her… yeah. I still would have taken her. For all I knew, the moment you drove away at her fake grave you were riding off and into your own. We thought… both of us thought you might be dead. I had to see it through. Get her to safety. It was the least I could do after how many times you've saved my ass."

"I'll never be able to repay you for this," Kye said, glancing at Eliana as she strapped on the helmet and mounted the back of his bike. "I'm here now, though. I can finish this last leg of the trip. When we hit the border, I don't want you to feel obligated to me anymore. Any debt between us is clear. You don't owe me anything."

"Shit, Kye," Grier said, removing his sunglasses entirely. "You think I'm doing all of this because I have some sense of obligation?" The two men stared hard at one another, and Kye nodded, feeling a lump in his throat.

"You've got your freedom now too; you can go wherever you like. Anyone looking for retribution or revenge will be on my ass, not yours. I'm not your president or your horseman anymore."

"No, but you're my friend, my brother; I'll see this through." They clasped hands, and Kye smiled.

"Love you too, brother," he said and gave Grier's cheek a light slap.

"Bastard," Grier chided, and they both laughed. "Get on your bike and take the lead. Your ol' lady is waiting for you."

"She sure is," Kye said more to himself than anyone as he moved back to his motorcycle. Eliana was sitting back on the seat, smiling from ear to ear. Holding a hand out to him, he took it and kissed her palm before placing her hand over his heart.

"Hi, baby," she greeted, her sparkling eyes sending a fresh wave of love and arousal through him. Taking her face in his hands, he gave her a firm kiss that spoke volumes of what he had intended for her in the near future. She shivered and took a sharp inhalation, her senses perking with desire.

"Let's go," he whispered against her lips. Taking his seat in front of her, the bike roared to life. The vibrations sent tremors through Eliana's legs and spine, and she tucked herself against Kye's back, his white cotton shirt soft against her chin as she rested it on his shoulder. He clicked on his helmet and pushed the kickstand up with his heel before launching them forward.

The roar of the bike echoed on the streets as Kye led the small convoy south. The wind whipped around them, and when they hit the open road, Eliana felt the rush of adrenaline mixed with the fresh and hot air that kissed her skin. She closed her eyes and smelled Kye's cologne, clean cotton shirt, sweat and the heat from the pavement. Her body came alive and with her arms stretched in the air, she felt bliss overtake her.

So, this is what Grier had been talking about... this wasn't peace. This was heaven.

* * *

"ALL SET," Grier said, walking out of the florescent-lit office of the one-story motel. He tossed a key ring with a single orange tag and key to Kye who caught it easily. "You're on the end, and I'm on the complete opposite side of the motel. Try not to need me for anything."

"Funny," Kye said, rolling his eyes and looking back at Eliana who was still resting on the back of his bike. The night was cloudy, and only the sparse streetlights illuminated the parking lot. Even still, he could see her beaming smile.

"Goodnight, Grier," she called to his retreating back. He lifted a hand in a single wave and disappeared behind the row of cars. Having made it safely to El Paso, they decided to stop for the night and cross the border in the early morning before it became too crowded.

"My lady," Kye said, extending a hand to her. Eliana looked back at him and took his outstretched hand.

"Ow!" she said with a chuckle as she dismounted. Taking her hand back, she rubbed her inner thighs. "How do you walk after riding all day?"

"You get used to it," Kye laughed as he watched her struggle to take a few steps.

"My thighs are on fire," she complained, but her face expressed amusement.

"Funny," Kye said, stepping closer and taking her arm, "mine too!" Slinging her arm over his head, he hoisted her over his shoulder.

"Kye!" she squealed and laughed when he gave her ass a hard smack. "What about my bag? I need my clothes!" Kye was already at the door to their room and with one hand unlocked the bolt and pushed the door open with his foot.

"Eli," he said, kicking the door shut and tossing her onto the bed, "for the next eight hours, there isn't a single article of clothing you'll be needing."

Eliana was biting her lip as she looked up at him, and Kye tugged his shirt off over his head. With the small amount of light that trickled through the thin curtains, she could see the shadows of the dark room washing over his ripped stomach. His defined chest rippled as he began unbuckling his belt, his slow and deliberate movements making her ache with desire.

His smooth skin was only tarnished with the occasional scar. Stories she would make him tell her one day. The bruising from his beating had mostly faded over the last few days, and the hungry look he was giving her spoke volumes of just how recovered he was.

When his pants hit the floor and he stepped out of them and his shoes in two quick movements, he was on her. Grabbing her by the ankles, he tore her boots off and yanked her pants down. Their earlier amusement had faded to carnal desire. Eliana sat up and pulled her shirt off. Before she could set to the task of unhooking her bra, Kye grabbed her by the front of it and hoisted her onto her knees.

Taking a fistful of her hair at the root, he yanked her head at a sharp angle to claim her mouth. She moaned, loving the way his warm body pressed against hers as he knelt on the bed in front of her. His free hand didn't waste any time as he dug in the front of her panties and slid two fingers between her folds. Her hips bucked at the sudden contact, and he sank his teeth into her bottom lip.

"Kye," she breathed when his mouth moved to her neck. He pulled back to look into her eyes, the dangerous expression making her wet. He was back at full force, and his focus was now entirely on her. "Don't hold back…"

"You asked," he said in a warning tone. She cocked her head to the side, challenging him with her eyes. He growled low in his throat and yanked her hips against his. The hardness of his erection pressed against her, and her legs involuntarily squeezed together.

His kiss was fierce, and her mouth was slow to keep

up with his insistent tongue. Her hands drew down his chest, running over the dusting of hair that ran down below his belly button. When she gripped him, he hissed a sharp breath and grabbed a handful of her ass. The grip he had was painful, but it sent shockwaves through her. The crack of a hard smack against her bare skin echoed in the room, and she gave a short yelp.

Her response was to grip him tighter and begin jerking her hand along his length. Kye grabbed the back of her bra and tore the hooks free. Her heavy breasts fell free, and he took a nipple between his teeth. Her cry was louder, and she dragged a hand through his hair. He took her firmly by the hips and flipped her around before pushing her onto her stomach.

The fabric of the comforter on the bed was scratchy against her skin, and her senses, which were on high alert, felt every strand of it beneath her. Kye hovered over her as he took in her bare back, carefully and painstakingly slowly pulling off her thong. When she lifted her hips to help them slide off easier, he jerked her backward, her knees tucking under her to elevate her backside.

Then his mouth was on her. Hot and aggressive, he tasted and lapped at her from behind. Her moan was guttural, and she buried her face in the pillows, eyes squeezed shut to savor every delicious flick of his tongue. Her legs were trembling already, and she was fast reaching a climax. Her body actively protested when he backed away. She moved backward hoping to find him, but he was already holding her hips, his erection fitting between her legs.

Kye didn't give her any time to adjust as he sheathed himself in one hard thrust. "Fuck," he groaned and pulled out of her only to slam back inside. The feel of his hardness inside her was bliss, and the way he relentlessly drove out and back in sent wave after wave of burning pleasure through her. Kye's breathing was heavy, and the way his shaft pulsed inside her slick heat made him lose himself.

He'd never taken her like this, and the feel of her tight ass against his pelvis, the way she pushed back against him craving him deeper inside, the way her walls clenched around him, drawing him in, he needed more. Sweat trickled down his chest, beading between his abdominal muscles, and the slap of their damp skin mixed with their passionate cries.

Kye was so deep inside her she could feel him hitting the opening to her womb inside. The stretching and ministrations were the perfect mix of pain and rapture. Her body seemed to react to everything he was doing, and when he gave her ass another hard smack of his hand, her back arched and he tugged on a handful of her hair until her throat was exposed and her breathing was forced into short rasps.

Though her position was one of complete submission, she did her best to draw her hips back. His pace was unyielding, however, and it was all she could do to brace herself on the bed and let him have his way. Breasts bouncing with the impact, she held herself up on her forearms, cheek pressed against the scratchy comforter. Even though he was using every inch of her body for his pleasure, he hadn't forgotten about her needs.

Kye's hand wound around her front to cup her clit, and with every thrust, it rubbed and drew tension against her most sensitive spot. Eliana's fingernails dug into his arm. The feeling of fullness combined with his firm hand against her sent her into climax. Her juices flowed over him, and the spasms of her body brought Kye with her.

Collapsing on top of her, his chest pressed against her back, he delicately removed himself and massaged her butt where a red handprint had formed. "Did I hurt you?" he asked as he kissed the back of her neck and pulled the sweaty hair away from her face.

"Mmhmm," she murmured in a lazy tone with a soft smile. She pressed her back more firmly against him. "And I hope you'll do it again soon."

12

_K_ye heard the shower running when he stepped back inside the motel room. He'd left early that morning on an errand with Grier and when he had, Eliana had been sleeping peacefully in the bed. It was a few hours later, the sun was up now, and he wasn't surprised she'd risen in his absence.

The sheets were still rumpled, and her clothes were strewn about. He'd left her bag just inside the door, and it lay open where she'd retrieved a clean set of clothes and her toiletries. Kye set the bag containing a fast-food breakfast and the cardboard carrying tray of coffee on the small end table and poked his head into the bathroom.

To his amusement, the room was full of steam from what must have been a blistering hot shower. He could barely make out her silhouette through the clear curtain.

Well, that wouldn't do. He gathered up the small pile that sat on the counter, tugged the towel off the rack, and slowly ducked back out.

A few minutes later he heard the water turn off. Sitting in the only chair in the room, he waited until he heard Eliana curse and step out into the room. Her eyes searched for a moment before landing on him. Her confusion turned into understanding, and she huffed.

"Good morning," he teased with a wiggle of his eyebrows. Her pile of clothing and the only towel sat on the floor next to him as he sat cross-legged in the chair. Eliana stood in the doorway to the bathroom dripping wet and entirely naked. His eyes raked over her shamelessly.

Her hair was even darker while it was wet, and his eyes followed a single drop of water as it fell from a strand of hair and cascaded down her bare chest between her breasts. Soft and pale, her two mounds came to shivering peaks with rosy pink nipples. Her soft areolas were pulled into taut peaks, small goosebumps marring her otherwise smooth complexion.

Her tiny waist came to a trim dip just under her ribcage, and her soft stomach had the right amount of plump to keep those hips full and fleshy. Her chest was rising and falling, her hands on those perfect hips as he devoured her with his eyes. Round hips gave way to full thighs, and her perfect v was covered in soft, trimmed hair that still glistened with water. He swallowed hard, his cock growing hard in his pants.

Her tender thighs stopped at two knees he'd since learned were ticklish on the underside. Kye had discovered this when they'd been draped over his shoulders the night before. Her smooth calves were slender, and her tiny, bony ankles had tasted salty when he'd kissed them. She was perfect.

Eliana moved toward him, and his legs uncrossed. She was biting her lip as she straddled him. His hands took her waist and traveled up her back and into her hair. God, she was good. She seemed just as aware of his body as he was of hers because the moment she was on him, her heat found the perfect spot over his cock to begin grinding against him. Her breasts were heaving in his face, and he kissed the tender skin.

"You took my clothes," she said, resting her arms on his shoulders. He grinned wickedly up at her.

"You look better without them," he admitted and lifted a hand to hold her left breast, the pink nipple staring at him mercilessly. He took it in his mouth and tugged on it with his teeth. She smelled fresh and soapy, and she tasted sweet. He was rewarded with a moan, and she wove a hand into his long hair. The bristles of his beard scratched at her tender skin.

"Mmm, is that coffee?" she asked teasingly as she leaned over to grab the Styrofoam cup. Kye growled as she took a long drink, her throat long and exposed as she tipped her head back. His hand wound around it, and he gripped her. She looked down at him with a raised eyebrow, and he took the coffee from her, setting it back down.

"You want your clothes back, you have to earn them," he said in a low voice. His hold on her throat was exciting. His dominance titillating. Her hand snaked between them, and she gripped his erection.

"Earn them? How would I do that?" she asked coyly as she massaged him through his jeans. He leaned forward and whispered in her ear, and she made a mock gasping noise. "You want me to what?" she asked in fake shock. "You're wicked."

"So are you," he agreed, grinding against her hand. She quickly unfastened his belt and withdrew him before she slid off his lap, dropped to her knees, and took him into her mouth.

* * *

ELIANA FINISHED off the last of her coffee that had long since gone cold from that morning. A faint smile still lingered on her face at the memory of their steamy morning. Now, Kye and Grier were settling matters with an overseer at the transportation depot just outside of the city near the border.

Kye's Harley and the Hummer were inspected and loaded onto a train that was due to leave within the hour. The haze and smoke that clouded the air from the coal train wafted in great billows. The overseer was a shorter man with a bald head and a dirty shirt, but he looked friendly enough. The three of them took turns shaking hands, a deal clearly struck, and both Kye and Grier made their way back over to her.

"So?" she asked, looking up at the two taller men.

"The train stops in Mexico City. Leon will see that the vehicles are on the exchange to get them into the country," Kye answered and wrapped an arm around her shoulders.

"We're catching the next bus out of town. We'll be out of the country in the next two hours," Grier said, unzipping the outer pocket of his backpack and removing three passports. He handed Kye and Eliana one, and she flipped hers open.

"Nancy Drew?" Eliana asked with narrowed eyes. The corner of Grier's mouth twitched upward ever so slightly.

"Yeah, you're both nosy and always getting into trouble," he said in a matter of fact tone.

"What's yours?" she asked, peeking at Kye's. He held it out to her, and she read the name. "Kyle Rayner? That's not very original."

"It's Green Lantern," Kye defended and pulled his fake passport back. Eliana rolled her eyes.

"I suppose you're Clark Kent?" she asked Grier who was pulling his sunglasses on and shook his head. "Thor?" Knowing Nancy Dre… er, Eliana wasn't going to relent, he handed his passport over. "Who's Dick Grayson?"

"Nightwing," Kye and Grier said simultaneously.

"Who's that?"

"Seriously?" Grier asked as though deeply offended. "Kye, your girlfriend needs a few valuable life lessons in comic book trivia."

"You know, come to think of it, 'Dick' is an excellent name for you, Grier," Eliana said flatly, and Kye laughed. He pulled her against his side as they set off for the other side of the transportation depot where the buses docked.

"Come on, baby," he said, kissing her temple, "by the time we get to Mexico, I'll have you all caught up on your comic book trivia."

"If Max is dead and you've paid the blood price to leave the Screaming Demons, why all the protocol? Why do we need to cross under assumed identities?" Eliana asked. She was grateful when they stepped into the air-conditioned station. Grier and Kye exchanged looks as they sat at the picnic-style table in the center of the room. Above them, the electronic board lit up with pending arrivals and departures. "What? What aren't you telling me?" Eliana asked when she noticed their unease.

"When an MC President…"

"Or Vice President," Grier added quickly.

"Or a Vice President," Kye agreed and continued his explanation, "leaves a club, especially a notorious one like the Screaming Demons, there is a level of risk that can befall them."

"How so?" Eliana questioned.

"Kye was an influential person, not just in the Demons," Grier said. "He's been involved in years of overseas operations and exchanges. There are a lot of smaller clubs that patched over to the Screaming Demons simply to avoid takeovers. Others, some regional clubs, lost a lot of profit because the Demons held a monopoly on gun trade in the northeast."

"Guns and drugs," Kye said, looking at Eliana with a steady gaze. She knew he was doing his best to be fully transparent with her. Though she didn't like hearing it, she appreciated that he was no longer hiding things from her.

"So… what? They're angry with you? They want to kill you or something?"

"Some, possibly," Kye answered, "what's likely happening, according to chatter, is that Grier and I have become what is known as an I.T."

"Let me guess, that doesn't mean 'information technology.'"

"Initiation Target," Grier replied.

"Or an Incentive Target," Kye added. "As former Demon officers, we have inside information that could either be seen as detrimental or incredibly helpful to other clubs. Especially those inside clubs that are looking to gain notoriety or status."

"Take out a former legend, become a legend yourself," Eliana concluded, and both men nodded. She buried her face in her hands for a moment then looked up at Grier, fearing the answer she may find in Kye's eyes. "Does it ever end? Are we going to be running forever?"

They were all quiet for a moment, and Kye reached over the table to take one of her hands in both of his. "No," Grier said, "not forever."

"You wouldn't lie to me," she said in a slightly warning tone, and he grinned.

"Dick Grayson doesn't lie," he teased, and she smiled. "It may be a few years, we'll need to stay low and keep quiet, but inevitably, eventually, the world will move on. Others will rise to power, make a name for themselves, and we'll be forgotten."

"You say that as though you're disappointed," she said as she'd noticed the forlorn tone and expression overtake his face.

"As much as I don't want to be assassinated, I don't like the idea of being forgotten," he replied, and Eliana felt she could empathize with that.

"Those that matter will always know who you are and that you matter," Eliana said gently. She reached her free hand out to lay on top of Grier's folded hands that rested on the table. The three of them sat like that for a long moment. Kye holding Eliana's hand, and Eliana holding both of Grier's. Their bond as a fast-formed family was sealed, and though in the last two months their entire world had been upheaved, they held a comradery that was unwavering.

"Now boarding the three o'clock bus to Monterrey. Please have your passports ready for the border crossing."

"Ready, Nancy?" Kye asked, standing and holding a hand out to her.

"I'm ready, Kyle," she answered back. Rounding the table, she took his hand and laced her fingers with his. She looked back over her shoulder at Grier who was still sitting at the table staring at something out the window. "Coming Grier?"

"Huh?" he asked, looking up. Shaking his head from his thoughts and glancing back at the figure he'd seen in the shadows, or at least one he thought he'd seen, and seeing there wasn't anyone there, he stood. "Yeah, I'm coming... I'm coming."

* * *

"Eli, wake up," Kye whispered as he gently shook her shoulder. Rolling her head away from the window of the bus it had been resting on, she could barely make out Kye's face in the darkness.

"What's wrong?" she asked, looking around. They'd been on the bus for over seven hours now. The border crossing had been nerve-wracking, but not a single guard had asked any questions about them or their passports. Grier had done an excellent job forging them. After darkness had fallen, Eliana had been unable to keep her eyes open as the bus hummed along on the two-lane highway and had fallen asleep. Now, it seemed much later in the night, the bus was at a complete standstill.

"Bus broke down," Kye said shortly, but there was something in his voice that made her nervous, and her senses perk up. "Grier went to talk to the driver; we've been sitting here for over an hour."

"Why didn't you wake me sooner?" she asked, sitting up fully and noticing Kye had draped his jacket over her.

"There wasn't any reason to do that. It seemed like it was just a flat tire."

"But now?"

"They've swapped the tire out, but we're still not moving."

"What does that mean?"

"I don't know," he said, trailing off as Grier made his way down the center aisle of the charter bus. "What did you find out?"

"The driver says its engine trouble. He called over the radio for another bus to come to pick us up, but he doesn't know how long that will take," Grier answered in a lowered tone of voice. Most of the passengers on the bus were asleep, and as the occupancy was almost at max capacity, it was better if it stayed quiet so the three of them could discuss their options.

"How far are we from Monterrey?" Eliana asked, sipping her bottled water. With the bus turned off, there was no air conditioning, and she quickly noticed how stuffy it was.

"He doesn't know. We're outside Santa Catarina that's for sure, but construction put us on a side highway."

"I don't like this," Kye said lowly as he watched the driver. The older man had shifty eyes, and he kept checking his phone and glancing back at them.

"Can we walk?" Eliana suggested, and they both looked at her. Kye and Grier had been thinking it but were unsure if she would be up for it.

"It's our best shot, but I don't want the driver knowing we've left until we're long gone. If he's helping someone track us, they'll be waiting in Monterrey at the bus station," Kye replied.

"Grab your stuff," Grier stated. He moved quickly down the aisle to the back of the bus and pushed on the bar to the emergency exit. An alarm blared loudly, and all the lights shot up.

"Que esta pasando?" someone yelled, and passengers began standing. Their panic was palpable and as they flooded the aisle, the driver began yelling instructions for them to remain seated.

"Come on," Kye said, taking her hand. They were ducked low and crawled out the side exit and ran across the road to the darkened side away from the lights of the bus. Grier caught up with them as they headed west and before long the bus was out of sight entirely.

"Are we sure that was a good idea?" he asked, and though he tried to keep it discreet, Eliana was positive she saw Grier hand Kye a pistol which he tucked in his belt under his shirt.

"Decision was made. Let's just get to Monterrey. We'll have to find another way into Belize, off of buses," Kye stated.

"Can't drive, can't ride the bus; we're running out of modes of transportation," Grier said, shouldering his backpack.

"If anyone can figure it out, it's you, Dick Grayson."

13

They'd been walking for close to three hours. According to Kye's watch, it would be dawn soon, and he'd hoped they'd reach a city before then. It would be easier to stay concealed at night, but luck wasn't on their side. Fortunately, the side roads they'd stuck to were mostly paved and easy to follow, especially with Eliana using the flashlight on her phone to lead the way.

He couldn't help but feel impressed with her. The Eliana who trekked five steps in front of them was not the fragile and vulnerable girl he'd met in high school and was definitely not the angry and frightened woman he'd kidnapped from her father's funeral all those weeks ago. Though still sparkling with that aura of beauty and radiance, she now had a fierceness she'd earned after weeks of surviving, seeing men die, and living on the run.

It was hot, even for being night. Temperatures were likely nearing the mid-nineties, and it would only get hotter when the sun rose, but she hadn't uttered a single complaint. The Eliana he'd known had always had a slight hesitation when it came to life and truly living. Though she'd never admitted it even to herself, she found comfort and safety in logic and in books. Maybe that was why she'd been drawn to the law; it was black and white and could easily be navigated to her. What she'd been living since he'd come back in her life could hardly fit that category.

Eliana had to learn about gray. There were crimes that were justified, like illegally crossing the border, and acts of virtue that had to be withheld, like turning criminals over to the police. Good guys didn't always do the right thing, and bad guys didn't always do the wrong. You couldn't always take life on its own terms; sometimes you had to live outside of the normal parameters to survive and to find yourself. These were all things Kye had discovered in his years with the MC, and he knew those lessons didn't come easily. He'd been afraid that as Eliana learned them, she'd lose herself.

Yet, here she was, leading them on their expedition on the deserted roads of Mexico toward freedom. Not only that, he could see the slight bounce in her step and the way she eagerly navigated them using the old fold-out map she'd taken from the bus depot before they left. She wasn't just participating in their adventure; she was enjoying herself.

"She's different," Kye said, feeling Grier walking next to him. In the dark, they couldn't make much out, but the two men stood close together for security.

"That's putting it mildly," Grier replied, and Kye could hear the smile in his voice. "She did well when you were gone. A royal pain in the ass half the time, never shutting up, but she did good. Followed instructions, for the most part, and had a good instinct about her. She'd have made a good ol' lady had things turned out differently."

"Yeah, she would have," Kye agreed. "Would you have stuck around the Demons had they not been trafficking girls?" he asked, seemingly out of nowhere.

"If you'd been in charge, you bet your ass I would have. Most of those guys, they were good, and the ride was a rush. I'm going to miss it, but I can tell you this, I won't miss Max or the politics. Things were getting scary during the last few years. People going missing. More Wall Kats showing up with bruises and brands. When I first joined, the club was about freedom. You could make something of yourself by doing your job and keeping your head down. Success was rewarded, and you could learn from the best. These last few years, though…"

"Go on," Kye encouraged.

"Things were different, man." Grier raked a hand through his hair. "It became less about the club and more about Max and his need for control. There was always this constant threat and fear riding under the surface. You never knew if you went out on a run if the guy at your side was going to be the one to put a knife in your back."

"It wasn't that way when we rode together. I always trusted you to have my back," Kye said.

"I always did have your back, and I knew you had mine; that's the club I was loyal to. That's what I'm going to miss. The rest of it can fuck off and die in my opinion." The two chuckled, and Eliana glanced over her shoulder at them. Kye tossed her a wink, and she was grateful it was dark enough he didn't see her blush. How the man could simply look at her and her knees went weak was completely unfair.

"I have a bad feeling about Monterrey," Kye said quietly and walked just a little slower to put some more room between them and Eliana.

"Yeah?"

"Yeah," Kye repeated. "I thought we were making the

safe choice skipping Mexico City and sending the vehicles on a separate route, but maybe it drew more attention to us."

"If there are bounty hunters after us, it won't matter what route we take. They're going to eventually find us. You weren't exactly low on the totem pole when it came to high mark hits. I know for a fact the Red Riders have had it out for you since you fucked over their opioid trade in Virginia."

"That's one of many, but I think they'll be top of the list. We need to keep an eye out for the Ace Jackets too. Peter and his old man tried to patch over in the summer, and I was instrumental in making sure that didn't happen," Kye admitted.

"Why did you do that?" Grier asked. The Ace Jackets were a mercenary club in Ohio that was notorious for the facial scars they left their enemies with.

"They had an in with Riggs. The last thing I wanted was him having more supporters if there was going to be any question who Max willed the club to when he died." Kye couldn't see him, but Grier nodded.

"Speaking of Max…" Grier trailed off, but Kye knew what he was asking.

"I'm still kicking myself for not checking for a pulse," Kye said sighing. "I've replayed the fight a million times in my mind, and I just can't come to an understanding. I don't know how he could have survived the cut to the eye, but I also know it wasn't fatally deep. I don't know why I held back. Max wouldn't have held back. He would have killed me had he gotten a better chance."

"Well, you're not Max," Grier said shortly. "You spent a lot of years trying to be him, to be just like him, but you've always been better. Whether he was trying to kill you or not, I think you still saw a sick and dying old man, and you couldn't bring yourself to murder him with a piece of broken glass."

"Maybe I did," Kye said, looking over at him. The full moon peeked out from behind a cloud, and he could just make out the side of Grier's face which seemed expressionless in the dark.

"Maybe you did; if we're lucky he's dead."

"What if he's not?"

"Then," Grier began as he shifted his backpack from one shoulder to the other, "you walked out of the club without being granted the blood price from the presiding president and shot one of his chief officers in the process."

"So, if he's not dead, we're completely fucked?"

"Yeah, pretty much."

"We're fucked," Grier repeated as he stepped into the cantina and slid into the seat next to Eliana.

"What, you can't find us a car?" she asked, knowing he'd just spent the last two hours trying to track one down for them.

"Oh no," he said, grabbing Kye's margarita and downing the rest of it. "Found plenty of cars, just no car services that will take us into Belize. It's too far."

"I'd like to say I'm surprised, but I'm not," Kye said, crossing his arms. "We've got almost thirty hours of road between us and there."

"So maybe we don't go to Belize," Eliana suggested. Kye and Grier both glared at her. "Just a suggestion…"

"Not a bad one," he said, taking her hand and kissing the back of it as a form of apology for his stern look. "But everything we need is there. It's one of the only safe houses I put a big stock of money into. The next closest one is just outside Belfast."

"That won't be an option then," she said, sighing. "We could fly," she offered. "Or take a boat?"

"A boat would take too long, and the waters are notorious for piracy. I don't think we can risk open water."

"So, we fly," she concluded.

"International airlines aren't an option," Grier said, exchanging the now empty margarita for Eliana's almost full one and sipping on it. "The moment we get into

TSA territory we are looking at facial recognition technology. Kye and I have managed to stay off of the FBI radar, but any entry-level hacker looking for us would be able to get access."

"Not to mention we're traveling with eight guns and half a million pesos," Kye added. "None of that is getting through airport security. What about the private sector?"

"As it happens, I looked into that," Grier said, wincing as the cheap tequila burned the back of his throat. "One of the drivers I spoke to suggested using his cousin's charter plane."

"You don't sound too confident," Eliana noted.

"I'm not," Grier confessed as he looked around for a waitress he could order another drink from. "I don't know shit about the guy and have no way to look into his credentials before we'd have to leave."

"What do you mean?" Kye asked, confused.

"The pilot, Alberto, is flying in from Coahuila today. He's stopping to refuel in town and then right back out to Ciudad del Carmen. The driver suggested we pay an extra ten thousand per person and he might take us on to San Pedro."

"That would put us only two hours outside Belize City," Eliana said, checking the map over. Kye's jaw clicked as it tensed.

"That's convenient," he said tersely.

"It seemed a little too convenient," Grier agreed.

"I think we should try it," Eliana said, folding the map up. "We can't be sure that this guy has bad intentions, and it seems the likely option he and his cousin just want to make some quick money. We pose as tourists looking to find a quick ride, they'll think nothing else. Bounty hunters can't have spies in every hangar in the world."

"She's got a point," Kye stated.

"Yeah, but we didn't survive this long taking unnecessary risks. We've always checked into our drivers and transports. We've never gone blind like this."

"We've never been forced to do any different," Kye countered. "We've had the luxury of time, but we don't have that now. I called the bus depot when you were out, and the bus we were stranded on never arrived. They sent the policia out looking for them."

"It's only been a few hours; let's not freak out just yet," Eliana advised, but even she had to admit she was feeling nervous. Once they were at Kye's safe house in Belize maybe she could breathe a little easier, but for now, her nerves were a half step away from frayed.

"Tell me about the plane," Kye said, rubbing his tired eyes. They'd been avoiding looking for a motel just yet, hoping they could catch a car out of town immediately, but it was looking more and more like they were going to be in town for several more hours. A little sleep wouldn't hurt.

"He said it was a turboprop aircraft, and freshly fueled it can take us to San Pedro with only one stopover. He said his cousin mainly uses it to deliver 'commodities', but it seats up to twelve passengers."

"Commodities?" Eliana asked and already knew the answer. Drugs.

"Does he have any passengers lined up? I don't want to be sharing the aircraft with anyone," Kye said, and Eliana had a feeling their plan was reluctantly coming into motion.

"He didn't say, just gave a price. Fifty thousand per seat."

"Pesos or American."

"Pesos."

"How did you swing that?" Kye asked incredulously. "They see an American and everything is in US dollars."

"I happen to speak flawless Spanish. As long as we keep our mouths shut, maybe we won't reek of American wealth," Grier stated.

"Right, let's not risk it. Tell him we'll pay seventy-five thousand up front and a hundred thousand upon arrival in Ciudad del Carmen. If he takes us on to San Pedro we'll pay fifty thousand for all three of us," Kye offered.

"These guys, they're going to want to see the money and credentials…"

"No," Kye said firmly. "Tell him you're representing a client who has special interests in some Honduran property and wants to keep a low profile so he's not bought out. If he doesn't accept that offer, an extra thousand pesos for his cooperation."

"If we throw too much money at them, they're going to milk us for more," Eliana added.

"I have no doubt, but if the worst should happen and they don't accept the offer, then we're right back where we started. We'll charter a car to take us to Belize in increments if needed," Kye said, and Grier nodded.

"Alright," he said, standing. "I'll take half the cash and pay up front; you keep the rest. If they kill me, at least you two should have the funds." He was only half-joking, and all three of them felt slightly nervous as they had to divvy the money into two smaller bags in the public location. Hoping they weren't seen, they agreed to meet back at this cantina in two hours.

"Where are we going?" Eliana asked as she fell in step with Kye as they left through the front door while Grier slipped out the back.

"There's a public market just down the road," he said, intertwining his fingers with hers. "If we're going to fool these guys into thinking we're property-hungry tourists, we need to look the part."

"Sunglasses and floppy hats?" she teased, and he gave her a tired smile.

"I'm going to buy you your first sombrero," he said and ruffled her hair. Eliana laughed and wrapped an arm around his waist. The beginning of the end was finally in sight.

"Alberto, estos son tus pasajeros," Diego, the driver that Grier had done all of his handlings with, introduced the three of them to their new pilot. The five of them were standing on the tarmac just outside the massive metal hangar. Diego had driven them there only thirty minutes ago, agreeing to make the introductions and leave them to their business. It had only cost five thousand pesos for his courtesy.

"Hola, amigos, es un buen dia para volar!" Alberto was a middle-aged man with a handsome face, dark brown skin and hair with flecks of gray at the temples. He shook Grier's hand firmly, then Kye's and when he took Eliana's he kissed the back of it.

"Es un muy buen," Grier replied. He hadn't been exaggerating. His Spanish was flawless, and he spoke it like he'd been born and raised south of the border. Just another element to his mystery, Eliana thought. "Cuando podemos esperar irnos?"

"I feel completely lost," Eliana said quietly, turning her back to the other men and looking up at Kye. He was dressed in a sexy white silk shirt with black embroidery, white slacks with dressy, but practical, shoes. His straw fedora was charming, and she saw her reflection in his sunglasses.

"He's asking when the pilot thinks he'll be ready to leave," Kye said, wrapping an arm around her. Eliana was comfortable in her light and airy red cotton dress that flowed around her ankles. When she placed a hand on Kye's shoulder, she caught sight of the beautiful opal charm bracelet he'd insisted on buying her.

"Cual es tu prisa, no te gusta Monterrey?" Alberto asked, and he and Diego laughed. Eliana sighed. She'd never been ungrateful for taking Latin and German for her foreign language credits until this moment. Though Latin was the root of many languages, she'd primarily studied the law terminology and somehow 'habeas corpus' didn't seem applicable at the moment. At least she hoped not.

"He's asking what our hurry is and if we don't like Monterrey," Kye translated in her ear. Though she hadn't heard him speak it yet, Eliana found it immensely sexy that Kye could speak the language.

"Mi esposa esta ansiosa por ver el oceana, Senor. Yo

estoy ansiosa por complacera," Kye said in accented but wonderful Spanish. Alberto laughed again and looked at Eliana with a crooked smile.

"That was sexy," she whispered, and he smiled down at her.

"I told him you were eager to see the ocean, and I was eager to see you pleased," he told her, and they both pretended not to watch as Grier opened his bag to pay Alberto.

"You wanna see me pleased?" she asked, looking at him over the top of her sunglasses. "Speak a little more of that Spanish and we can join the mile-high club." Her wink and suggestion sent a jolt of arousal through him, and Kye had to force his mind to stay focused on their task. He pretended to stretch and take a few steps away from them as he surveyed the landing strip.

It wasn't a fully private airport, but it definitely wasn't run by the government. He could see inside the hangar several charter planes, small passenger jets, and a few turbo planes for crop dusting were housed, but at the moment there were no aircraft flying overhead. The fact that the place wasn't too busy was both a blessing and a curse. While it would likely afford them an earlier departure time because they wouldn't have to navigate air traffic, it would also be easier for someone to track down their flight if they were looking for them.

"We're all squared," Grier said, walking over to him.

Alberto and Diego were chatting and laughing like the best of friends, probably elated to have found such stupid Americans to pay so much for a four-hour flight. "He said it'll take a few hours to refuel and have the plane emptied, but we should be able to leave before nightfall."

"That's good," Kye said with his arm still protectively wrapped around Eliana. "It's been twenty hours since we left the bus on the side of the road. I want to be out of town before tomorrow. Do we have somewhere we can lay low until the plane is ready?"

"I say we arm up, get a hot meal, and get back here just before he leaves. The longer we linger the more attention we draw," Grier said, noticing the way the airport workers all stared at the wealthy-looking Americans.

"Good idea. Can Diego give us a ride back to town?" Kye asked, knowing they were thirty minutes from the downtown district they'd left.

"I'm sure he can, he already offered to bring us back when Alberto is ready. I have a feeling they don't want us seeing what they're unloading or loading," Grier stated. Eliana felt a shiver run down her spine at the thought.

"It's okay," Kye said, sensing her fear. "In two hours, we're out of here. Did Alberto agree to fly us on to San Pedro?"

"He was ready to fly us to the moon for more money," Grier said dryly. "Come on, I'm famished, and I need a drink."

"When do you not need a drink?" Eliana asked sarcastically.

"When I have a full one in my hand," he retorted, and she snorted out a laugh.

* * *

"THIS IS TAKING TOO LONG," Eliana said nervously as she wrung her hands in her lap. They were sitting in the back of Diego's town car, and though they'd been promised a departure before sunset, the burning orb was low on the horizon, and they hadn't heard anything from the pilot since that afternoon.

"I'm going to check," Grier said from the front seat and stepped out of the car. Diego had picked them up at the restaurant they'd eaten at, and though all three of them were secretly armed, Eliana didn't feel safe in that moment.

The airport had been buzzing with activity earlier in the day. Workers running to and fro with fueling hoses, cleaning equipment, carts of luggage and crates, and even a few guys with those light-up sticks that helped direct traffic. Now the whole place was dead. Only the plane they knew belonged to Alberto was sitting in wait for liftoff, and the only lights they could see were the blue runway lights, a red flickering one from the tower in the distance, and the flood of light from inside the hangar that was nearly fifty yards away.

"There they are," Kye said, pointing. Grier was only a few steps outside the vehicle when Diego and Alberto were seen walking toward them from the hangar. As they drew closer, Kye stepped out of the car first and signaled for Eliana to wait. The four men exchanged handshakes quickly.

"My apologies," Alberto said in hurried Spanish. He seemed flustered, and that immediately sent Kye and Grier into hyperawareness. "It took longer to refuel than expected. The engine is warming up, and we will leave soon. My cousin can show you onto the plane."

"Thank you," Kye said and turned to wave for Eliana to join then, but Alberto stopped him.

"Before we go, I must ask that you allow me to search your belongings." Kye froze.

"Why?" he asked in a stern voice.

"Please, I am responsible for whatever items come onto my plane. If you have any weapons or contraband, I need to know about it," Alberto defended. His forehead was sweaty, and neither Kye nor Grier figured it was because of the sweltering heat.

"Only our guard is armed," Kye said, gesturing to

Grier he patted a hand on the gun he openly wore on his hip. "I don't carry, and my wife hates guns."

"Women," Diego said in a joking manner, trying to lighten the mood. It didn't work.

"I respect your answer. If your guard can hand over his weapon, I will see it will be returned once we arrive."

"No…" Grier began, but Kye held a hand up.

"Agreed, we need to have trust between us, right?" Kye asked, hoping to keep things from escalating. These men were nervous, and that made them dangerous.

"We must also still search your things," Alberto said, taking the gun Grier handed him. Though he'd passed it over, Grier was sure to remove the clip and tuck it into his pocket. He wasn't about to hand over a loaded weapon.

"What about trust, sir?" Kye asked, crossing his arms.

"Please, understand," Alberto pleaded with a soft smile. Kye stared at him hard for a moment, but the longer they lingered the worse this would get.

"Alright," he relented, and he felt Grier tense up next to him. Diego moved quickly to the trunk and removed the three bags that they'd brought. The first contained mostly Eliana's things, the second was the bag with cash, and the third held their documents, Grier's clothing, and a few stashed souvenirs.

"You see?" Kye asked, smiling. "We have nothing to hide."

"You travel with a lot of money," Diego said, shouldering their bags and closing the trunk.

"As we stated, I plan to buy some property. I find that having money makes that easier." Alberto and Diego laughed, and it sounded oddly relieved. Perhaps the two men were nervous thinking they were being set up.

"I think we can trust you; you are good, honest men," Alberto said, handing Grier the gun back. "I only ask you keep it unloaded while we're in the air. Should it accidentally go off, we will lose cabin pressure."

"Of course," Grier said and was happy to have his sidearm back. The four men were collectively breathing a sigh of relief, and Kye had just opened the door to let Eliana out when the squeal of tires shattered their moment of relaxation.

"Run!" Diego yelled, and none of them were quite sure who it was to. A black Jeep tore out of the hangar, and sprays of gunfire lit up the imposing night.

"To the plane!" Alberto cried. Kye grabbed Eliana by the arm and half dragged her toward the aircraft. Grier was laying down cover fire, but the machine gun mounted on top of the roofless Jeep was firing much faster. The three of them were forced to duck behind the town car that was peppered with bullets.

"Who are they?" Eliana asked, fear seizing her. Alberto had managed to make it to the plane, but Diego was crouched with them speaking in such frenzied Spanish; even Grier couldn't understand him.

"Right now, they're the guys trying to kill us," Grier said, standing for a brief moment to shoot off a few rounds at the Jeep that was nearing them. He ducked just in time as the window next to him shattered.

"Come here," Kye said, grabbing at Eliana. She lifted the bottom of her dress, and Diego shouted, clearly unsure what they were doing. That was until he saw the four leg holsters she was wearing under her flowing dress. Two guns on either leg, one on each thigh and calf, she'd been hiding the weapons on her person just in case their bags were searched.

Kye tossed one of them to Grier who quickly reloaded, then took two for himself. "We're going to lay down a shit ton of fire; you run like hell to the plane," he instructed Eliana. She shook her head.

"You're not sending me away," she protested. He quickly kissed her forehead.

"I'm right behind you this time. Just keep Alberto from taking off until we're there," he said firmly. Eliana only nodded. "Three, two, one, go!" he shouted. She didn't hesitate. As Grier and Kye stood, using the car to shield them, they fired almighty hell at the oncoming vehicle, and Eliana bolted.

She could feel Diego on her heels, but didn't stop to look. Her eyes were fixed on the lowered staircase that led up to the plane. Her hand had just reached the railing when she heard the impact of a bullet on skin. She froze and looked down. Diego, who'd been just behind her, had taken a bullet to the back of the head. It had made a sickening cracking sound when it entered his skull, and he lay on the ground at her feet, very much dead.

"Go, Eli!" Kye shouted. Her mind was blank, but her instincts were on point. She grabbed the bags off Diego's dead body and tossed them into the open door of the plane that was now roaring to life. She watched, terrified, as the Jeep with three surviving black-clad occupants reached the town car.

Kye was crouched reloading his gun when the Jeep reached them. The car was hissing and smoking as bullets had shattered the radiator and all the windows. Grier jumped out from behind the trunk and took down two of the gunmen. Kye had only just chambered his clip when a man wearing a black bandana over his mouth came around to his side of the car.

"Drop it!" he said in English, aiming a gun at Kye. Without any time to respond, the man cried out as a bullet hit him, and he fell to the ground. Kye stood in shock as he saw Eliana standing with her own smoking weapon drawn.

"You shot him..." Kye said, bewildered. She looked terrifying at that moment. Eyes wild and cheeks flushed.

He only snapped to attention in time to tackle her as more shots rang out. A second and a third Jeep were racing toward them. "Go, go, go!" Kye shouted. He snatched up the fallen man's automatic gun and fired it toward the Jeeps as Grier and Eliana sprinted up the steps to the plane.

They were barely on board when its wheels began to move. Eliana pushed past Grier to the open door as she watched Kye still firing from the ground.

"Kye!" she screamed in complete terror. He looked over his shoulder and saw the plane was moving. He cursed and ran after them. Grier pushed her aside and fired off cover fire for his friend, who was running full speed trying to get to them.

Eliana was screaming at Alberto to wait, but he either wasn't listening or didn't understand. She could still hear gunfire, but couldn't see anything as Grier's body took up the whole doorway.

"Please, please!" she cried, hot tears pouring out of her eyes. "Don't leave him!" When the plane jerked upward, its wheels now off the ground, Eliana collapsed in a heap on the floor and screamed in rage and adrenaline.

"It's okay, it's okay! Help me!" Grier called in a strangled voice. She looked up and saw him half in the doorway and half inside. With one arm he was clinging to the seat closest to him and with the other, he was tugging on something. Eliana scrambled to her feet and when she reached him, she saw he was holding onto Kye's arm as he clung to the staircase railing.

Together, they hoisted him inside, and he collapsed onto Eliana. Grier quickly used the rope to pull the door shut and seal it before the plane got too high. "Are you okay?" Kye asked, looking down at her. They were both shaking, and she had her eyes closed tightly.

"I thought… I thought…"

"Shh…" he soothed and sat back to pull her into his arms. "I'm here. We're okay. We made it. We're safe."

Though he spoke the words, his eyes looked up at Grier, and they both silently asked one another the same questions: Were they safe? Who were those men?

15

Alberto had straight up refused to take them on to San Pedro so it was another six hours of travel after they landed. Though still reeling from their shootout, Eliana was grateful to be on the ground. She felt helpless up in the air. Should the worse come to it, there wouldn't be anywhere to run when you were a few thousand feet off the ground. At least driving they had options for places to run.

Finally, inside the boundaries of Belize, Kye was driving the rented BMW he'd acquired under his assumed identity. Still too jittery to sleep, the three of them alternated between pensive silence and restless discussion. They'd all hoped once they were in Mexico, whoever might be trailing them would back off, but clearly vehicles full of armed, masked men spoke otherwise.

"I didn't think anything of it at the time," Grier said as the topic came up on who may be pursuing them, "but when we were at the bus depot, I swore I saw someone…"

"Who?" Eliana asked from the backseat. She was fairly certain she'd been dozing for the last hour, but was wide awake now.

"I don't know. I mean, there were a lot of people in and out. As I said, I didn't think much of it, but they were a rider. All black riding leathers and helmet. It didn't look like he was watching us, but… Shit, after what we just survived, I can't get it out of my mind," Grier said, raking his hands through his hair. He sounded more tired than ever before.

"Could be related, but there's nothing we can do about it now," Kye said, turning off the main road to a slower two-lane street. The area they were entering was residential, but they were well inside the Sibun Forest Reserve, and the scenery was quickly fading from populated to tropical scenery. Its beauty was evident, but it all seemed to pass as a blur outside the window. "Whoever was at the airport already knew we were in town if they'd tracked us from the bus depot. We just have to hope they don't know where Alberto dropped us."

"He sure didn't stick around long. He might as well have pushed us out the door, he took off so fast after we landed," Eliana said, stretching. She caught Kye looking at her in the rearview mirror, and she smiled at him.

"He probably carried on to Campeche or headed back west. A smaller plane like that wouldn't be able to last much longer in the air without refueling," Grier commented.

"I'm not convinced those men were specifically after us," Eliana said, "Diego and Alberto were already acting nervous, they were running behind schedule, and were known to smuggle items in and out of the country. For all we know, they were local thugs looking to make a heist."

"I won't disagree with that theory," Kye said, gripping the wheel a little tighter. "Better to be safe than sorry, for now. We'll get to the safe house and lay low for a bit then discreetly put some feelers out and try to get some answers." They all nodded their agreement.

The road they were on took a sharp turn after a fork, and Kye took the road that was unpaved. The red dirt kicked up around them, and the car slowed to a more manageable pace.

"How do you know where we're going?" Eliana asked, leaning over the center console to look out through the windshield.

"I've driven this road once or twice," he said, grinning at her. "Probably a thousand times in my mind.

This has always been the endgame, baby, taking you here when things were safe, and we could be together."

"Who's the bigger third wheel, me or the thugs following us?" Grier asked, rolling his head to look over at them.

"Aww," Eliana teased and wrapped an arm around his shoulders and planted a kiss on his cheek. "We like you, Grier. You're not a third wheel."

"Gee, thanks," he said sarcastically and wiped his cheek where she'd kissed him. Kye felt a fleeting moment of jealousy, but when he squelched it, he came to a level of gratefulness that his girl and his best friend had formed such a fast bond.

"We'll be there soon," Kye said, and the three fell into silence again. Eliana sat back and watched the scenery pass by the window.

The tropical vibe was everything she remembered from her adventurous spring break trip. The towering palms and mangrove trees were flourishing, and the lower to the ground bushes were ornamented with red and yellow flowers. That was the extent of the similarities, though. When she'd gone with her friends, they'd stayed in the heart of Belize City. Now, they were farther south, and the landscape was much less touristy and populated.

They had been driving on the same red dirt road for nearly forty minutes when she saw the first signs of a structure. A twenty-foot wall of cream-colored cement topped with barbed wire opened only far enough for a wooden gate with metal plating. Kye left the car running as he hopped out and walked to the gate. Pulling a keychain from his pocket, he unlocked the chain and yanked the gate open wide enough for them to pass through. Once they drove through, he was sure to close it behind them before they continued on.

"Were those cameras?" Eliana asked, noticing the devices topping the wall.

"They won't be on yet," Kye answered. The road narrowed, tall trees on either side of the street that looked more like a footpath now. "Welcome home," Kye said when the forest opened up into a circular driveway.

In the center of the roundabout was a three-tiered fountain, but it wasn't currently running. The road turned to gray cobblestones that had three adjoining paths. Kye pulled the car to a stop in the center, and they all slowly climbed out. Eliana's eyes devoured everything, trying to take it all in.

When Kye had said they were going to a safe house, she imagined something like the old barn that she and Grier had switched vehicles at. What she was looking at was hardly a debilitated barn. It was a mansion built directly into the forest. Straight ahead of them was a two-story building with an A-frame thatch roof with open rafters.

The second story looked to be made entirely of windows and was surrounded by a wrap-around deck. The main floor had open archways for doors, and the building seemed to glow a vibrant yellow in the afternoon sun.

Kye and Grier were taking the path toward the main house, and she followed slowly behind them. The path to her left seemed to disappear in a downhill direction that she couldn't see beyond, but the path to her far right led to a long one-story building that looked like a former stable.

Kye and Grier had already entered the house, and Eliana jogged to catch up. It was hot outside, probably mid-eighties, but inside seemed cooler with the open windows granting a constant breeze. The front foyer was small but opened to both a living room and casual dining room, and the far end was a kitchen partially walled off by an island and a bar. The hardwood floors were smooth and had a slightly red tinge to the wood. The walls and portions of ceiling that weren't open to the rafters above were trimmed in white, and yellow paper lanterns hung like ornaments.

Grier was making his way upstairs, the steps lined with a branch-like railing, and Kye was yanking the tarped sheets off of the furniture. Though she couldn't imagine it was the type of house that got dusty, when she saw the wood furniture that was covered in brightly colored cushions, she assumed they were to protect from sun damage.

"There's a bathroom down that hall, or there are two upstairs. One off the main hallway or one through the master bedroom," Kye said as he tossed the sheets over the back of an armchair. He crossed the room and wrapped his arms around her, hoisting her off her feet. "How do you like it?"

"This place is amazing," she said, stroking his hair and smiling down at him as he held her tightly against his chest.

"Think it is somewhere you could be happy?" His blue eyes, though tired, were full of optimism and a kind of hope she hadn't seen in him since high school.

"If I'm with you, I'm happy," she said softly, resting her hand against his cheek. Kye smiled and slowly lowered her, catching her lips as he did. Their kiss was powerful and searing. He cupped the back of her head with both hands, and she melted against him. All the fear of the last few days faded as they embraced each other.

"The hot water should be working," he said, pressing his forehead against hers. I'm going to run into town, pick up a few things. Why don't you get cleaned up and rest?"

"Mmm," she said with a pouting lip. "I don't want you to go." Kye chuckled and kissed her forehead.

"You will in about an hour when you get hungry and there's no food in the house," he reasoned. "Besides, the town is only about twenty minutes from here, and I'll be back soon. Trust me, I'm ready to be here and rest with you, but we can't do that if we're all starving. Grier is going to get started setting up the security system and after that…" He trailed off and kissed her again.

"Hurry back," she whispered against his lips, and he smiled, kissed the back of her hand, and left.

Eliana took a moment to look over the house once more before making her way upstairs. For the first time in… she couldn't even recall, she felt safe and happy.

* * *

THE FIRE in the stone pit crackled, and three sets of eyes stared into it. Grier, Eliana, and Kye were sitting on the back deck next to the empty pool, each nursing a beer and resting contentedly in the reclining deck chairs. The sun had set hours ago and though they were tired, none of them were going to miss out on savoring their first night in freedom.

Grier had gotten the security system running in a matter of minutes. As it turned out, the entire compound, including the main house, stables, and six on-campus shacks and a fishing dock, were all walled in. The twenty-foot cement wall was reinforced with copper bars, barbed wire, and an interior electric fence. Rotating cameras were placed every ten feet and were linked to the floodlights. Should the sensors catch something, the entire place would light up and alarms would sound.

When Kye had been out buying groceries, including the hot dogs and beer they were enjoying for dinner, Grier had shown her the floor level armory that had once been designed as a pantry, as well as the two removable walls upstairs that pressed in to reveal a gun stash and a panic room. If that wasn't enough, both men were already discussing the security teams they were going to put together.

"I say we reach out to the Houston Bells," Grier suggested as he passed Kye another beer. "They've got a whole chapter of former military contractors that could be looking for work."

"Former military? Like Dhal?" Eliana asked nervously and looked over at Kye. They were lying together on one of the lounge chairs, and he kissed the top of her head.

"No, baby," he said reassuringly. "No one like Dhal. That crazy motherfucker got what he deserved."

"Less than," she muttered and hugged him closer.

"We've got a few days to think it over," Kye said, downing a mouthful of his beer. He grew quiet and stared into the fire. Eliana was already closing her eyes and barely holding onto consciousness as she lay her head on Kye's chest.

"I'm off to bed," Grier said, standing. He was a little unsteady on his feet, having polished off his fourth beer, and Kye chuckled. "Try to keep the moaning to a minimum. I think I've earned a good night's rest."

"Goodnight!" Eliana called without opening her eyes, which meant she missed the one-finger salute Kye threw at Grier. When he was inside and upstairs, Eliana cracked her eyes open and looked up at Kye. He was laying with one arm tucked behind his head, eyes staring up at the sky.

"Beautiful, isn't it?" he said, beckoning her to join his stargazing. Eliana, however, couldn't take her eyes off of Kye. She smiled and traced a finger over the scar under his eyebrow. Kye glanced down at her and smiled softly, his hand running up her back to stroke her hair.

"This place is beautiful, Kye," she said, making small circles on the exposed skin of his chest just below his throat.

"It'll be better once we get the place up and running. We'll get the pool filled and maybe spruce up the garden. Tomorrow I can take you down to the dock. It's small, but if you've never been fishing before…" His sentence was cut short as she scooted up just enough to kiss him.

Her kiss was firm but tender, and she held his face with both hands, her tongue drawing lazily over his bottom lip. Kye smiled and brought her up until she was lying fully on top of him. "I love you," he said, pressing their foreheads together. She smiled, her thumb pressing his chin.

"I love you too. I think we're going to be happy here… I want us to be happy here," she said with a level of vulnerability she didn't know she still had. The last few weeks had made her hard, both mentally and emotionally; she felt shut down. But now, as they lay there, pressed together next to the fire under the starlight, her walls were coming down again.

"We will be happy here, I promise," Kye said gently. "I'll make you happy. For the rest of my life, I'll do everything I can to make you happy. We can put all this chaos and fear and violence behind us."

"I promise the same thing," she said, shifting on top of him so she could look into his eyes better. "I think we both deserve a little happiness after everything."

"Agreed," Kye said chuckling. His hands were rubbing her back, and the gesture made her relax into him. With her head on his chest again, they both, for the first time in ages, simply held each other while they slept in perfect blissful peace.

$\mathcal{E}$liana woke the moment she felt his hands between her legs. Her back was facing him, her face partially buried in the thick and soft down pillows. Kye's erection was already pressing against her back, and the way he rocked his hips against her ass pulled her from her slumber. Smiling, she turned her head to the side, and his mouth was on her.

The scratchy texture of his growing beard felt stimulating against her soft skin. His hand was cupping her heat, and she ground against it. They'd been at it most of the night and clearly, neither of them were satiated. As the predawn sky began to lighten, birds waking from their peaceful sleep and chirping happily, Eliana rolled the rest of the way over until she was straddling his hips.

Kye's eyes went wide; clearly, he hadn't been expecting that, and when, in one swift drop, she claimed him inside her, his groan sent shivers up her spine. Her slick heat was already aroused, their night of passionate love-making still lingered in the air, and her skin was prickling with desire as she rocked her hips against his.

Seemingly liking the dominant position, when Kye reached to cup her bare breasts, neither of them seeing any reason to wear clothing to bed anymore, she firmly took his wrists and pinned them above his head. Her pelvis tipping forward, his hipbone rubbed her clitoris, and she cried out in pleasure. Her grip on his wrists tightened, her thighs squeezing him, her walls clamping down on his shaft, her orgasm was swift and powerful, and she shook for a long time, riding the waves of ecstasy as they surged from head to toe.

Kye couldn't resist any longer and took her hips, driving her back down, and his hips rose to meet her. Though sensitive and reeling, the feel of him strong and hard inside her was so enjoyable, she didn't care that he was plundering her cave with the ferocity of a jackhammer. Kye's upward strokes were so robust, her breasts bounced and she had to grip the headboard to steady herself.

Knowing she was no delicate flower, Kye took his pleasure in her. She rode him, matching every single one of his bucks and humps like the best of the rodeo champs. Trying to get a better angle, he rolled her onto her back and yanked one of her legs over his shoulder before reentering her. Eliana was biting her lips so hard she was sure she tasted blood, but the mixture of pain and pleasure was so liberating she couldn't care less if she bit her own lip off.

Kye burst over the edge, his climax shooting so forcefully inside of her that she trembled again, his throbs matching her pulses. He lay on her stomach, forehead sweating and hair damp with perspiration. She stroked the wet strands away from his face, and he smiled as he nuzzled between her breasts, peppering the tender undersides with kisses.

"Good morning," he said, still slightly out of breath. Eliana giggled and moved to massage his broad shoulders.

"Morning," she greeted in blissful and relaxed contentment. "Are you hungry?" she asked after she felt his breathing return to normal.

"Famished," he admitted. All their cardio was working up quite the appetite.

"Hela is coming over today. I promised her we'd talk over her situation." Kye made a noise of understanding before he rolled over so she could look in his eyes.

"Her husband didn't sign the papers, did he?" Kye asked and couldn't help but play with the two mounds of flesh that were resting in his face. Eliana squirmed under the pressure of his thumbs on her nipples.

"No, he's being difficult. He doesn't want to pay child

support, so he's trying to draw things out until she runs out of money," Eliana said, sighing in frustration. Hela, one of the local shop owners, had become a good friend of hers in the last few months, and Eliana had since learned that Hela's husband was divorcing her and, as she was fairly poor, didn't have the money for a lawyer. Eliana had agreed to do it for free.

"You'll think of something, baby," Kye said, propping himself up on his forearms and kissing her. "Are you going to stop by the shop today?"

"Don't I always?" she asked in a teasing tone as she stroked his face. She decided she liked his beard. He kept it trimmed and soft, and it made him look rugged and, if possible, more handsome than ever.

"Good," he said, grinning and kissing her. His semi-returned erection pressed against her wet folds, and she made an involuntary jerking motion. They both laughed as he tossed the covers over them, and they went at it again.

"Good morning, Matty!" Eliana called as she waved to the man on the far side of the compound. The medium height man with a rippling upper body and thick thighs was dressed in his usual khaki-colored cargo pants and a fitted muscle shirt. Carrying a semi-automatic gun, he waved to her. "I brought lunch," Eliana said and handed him the white cloth wrapped sack of food. Containing a fish sandwich, a papaya, and two freshly baked cookies, Matty shouldered his weapon and took it gratefully.

"Thank you, ma'am," he said, accepting it. Eliana reached back into her brown wicker basket and retrieved an ice-cold bottle of soda.

"Don't forget we're having the fish fry on Saturday. I want you to bring your wife and son," Eliana said, pointing at him with an almost accusatory finger.

"I promise!" Matty said, holding up his right hand as though taking a solemn vow. Eliana smiled and waved as she continued along the path that encircled the compound.

It had been nearly six months to the day since they'd arrived in Belize. Eliana felt immense satisfaction in the routines she'd built for herself. It was easier to find things to do now that there were more people living on the compound with them. True to their plan, Grier and Kye had recruited some patch brothers from clubs in the south, primarily Texas, to come and work for them.

Among them were Matty, the security sergeant who lived off-site with his pregnant wife and three-year-old son, and four others. Luca was a quiet man with ashy blonde hair and tattoos on his arms who'd served four tours overseas with both the Army and the Air Force at one point. He worked primarily in the control room monitoring the cameras. He lived off-site too and was rumored to be dating a local woman. Then there were the brothers, Douglas and Russell, both former Marines who patrolled their beachfront and dock, lived in the shacks down the way from the main house. They'd fixed them up like cabanas and liked to shoot the shit with Grier.

It had taken much convincing for Grier to stay on. Not that they hadn't asked him a million times their first few weeks, Grier seemed reluctant to agree. Maybe he thought he was imposing on their happily ever after or whatever, but it had come down to both Kye and Eliana sitting him down and telling him how much safer they both felt with him around. When they agreed to let him pick his own crew and open up a bar off-site, he'd finally unpacked his bag. Eliana was ecstatic he'd decided to remain in the main house with them but insisted he needed to renovate the downstairs office into a bedroom with a private entrance. Mainly because it was as far away from Kye and Eliana's master suite as possible.

In desperate need of some estrogen, Eliana had formed several friendships with the women in the nearby village. Her Spanish was still rusty, but she was learning quickly. Hela owned a salon and boutique off the main road. Though it was small, Hela designed and made most of the clothes she sold and was actually very talented at cutting and styling hair. Eliana made it a habit to get her hair treated every two weeks. Not that she was going to complain about that. Her previously short locks were now wistfully flowing down the middle of her back.

Hela was also helping Eliana practice her Spanish. The woman, in her mid-thirties, was dark-skinned with shimmering brown hair and eyes the color of honey. How her bastard of a husband could justify cheating and divorcing such a sweet, beautiful, intelligent and funny woman was beyond anything Eliana could understand. Even when Eliana wasn't getting her hair done, the two would often sit out front of her shop drinking coffee and laughing at the children who played in the streets.

Belize life was very different than American. There was no sense of urgency or panic. No one was in a hurry, and no one ever seemed angry; except maybe a few of the men who frequented Grier's bar for soccer games. Their rowdy chants and aggressive boos when their team was losing could be heard for miles.

It was easy for Eliana to slip into a comfortable life. She would spend her mornings in bed with Kye, then she'd clean and maintain the house while he went off to work the mechanic shop he'd opened in the old stables on the compound premises. She'd cook lunch for all the guys and take a nice long walk to deliver the food and cold drinks before eating lunch with Kye every day.

Twice a week Eliana would work with Russell and Douglas to practice shooting or kickboxing. In the evening, those who lived on-site would gather at the main house or off the dock for beers and a bonfire. A few times a week they'd go out to Grier's bar, and every Sunday Eliana and Kye would spend the whole day riding up and down the coast on his Harley that had arrived in Belize shortly after they had.

Things were perfect. For the most part.

"Hi, baby," Kye greeted. He was working on an old farming truck a local had brought in. He was bare-chested, and his work overalls hung low on his hips, torso stretched and muscles rippling as he reached overhead to loosen something just under the front axle.

"Hey there, sexy man," she greeted and stood on her tiptoes to kiss his cheek from behind and gave his earlobe a flirtatious bite.

"Oh," Kye said, leaning into it. The small gesture made his cock twitch. "Are you sure we can't lift that ban on sex in the shop?" he asked, setting his socket wrench down and turning to look at her. Eliana was dressed in a turquoise blue dress with a bright yellow necklace. Her bare arms crossed over her chest.

"Since the last time when Luca walked in on us thinking someone was beating me, no, dear, we cannot lift the ban," she said in a much more serious tone than she actually felt. Kye sighed dramatically and kissed her.

"I'll settle for lunch then," he said and went to wash his hands as she laid out the food on the small table next to his workbench. Soft but lively music was playing over the radio and when Kye returned from the bathroom, he'd pulled a white shirt on. "This looks good," he complimented as he surveyed the sandwiches, fruit, and drinks.

"Thank you," she said proudly, and they both began to eat. "How's work?" she asked, glancing at the truck that was dripping blue fluid.

"Eh," Kye said, shrugging, "mostly road damage, shouldn't take long. Told the farmer I'd cut him a deal if he agreed to send us a shipment of the potatoes he's growing."

"Quite the entrepreneur," she teased, and Kye shrugged again.

"It's not like we need the money," he said, taking another bite and speaking with a full mouth. "I just work to keep busy."

"I know," Eliana said and started picking at her sandwich, her eyes falling to the table.

"Something is wrong," Kye said, noticing her change in expression. "Everything okay with Hela?"

"No worse than before," Eliana set her food down. "It's just that, you know I went into town earlier…"

"Did you see something?" Kye asked with a sudden hint of paranoia. While they were comfortable in their slice of heaven, none of them ever forgot they could still be in danger.

"No, no, nothing like that," Eliana said but still didn't meet his eyes. "I just, you know…" She was having a hard time finding her words, and Kye, sensing this, set his crust aside and took her hand.

"Tell me."

"I went to see the local physician today. Nothing serious, just a check-up. Women's stuff and all that…"

"Did the doctor find something? Are you sick?" She gave him an annoyed look. His insistence wasn't helping her retell her story. "Are you pregnant?" he asked suddenly, eyes as wide as a deer in headlights.

"God, no, Kye I'm not pregnant…"

"Thank God!" he said, sitting back in his chair and clutching a hand to his heart. Eliana was more annoyed than ever.

"Well, she did ask if I needed a refill of birth control. I told her I needed to think about it, but I guess that answers the question!" she snapped and stood. Before she made it two steps, Kye caught her arm.

"Hey, wait," he said, pulling her back. "I didn't mean it like that. I just… I don't want to accidentally bring kids in the world. If… I mean, when we decide to have children, I want it to be because we both agree, not because we weren't being careful."

"I can agree with that," Eliana said, letting him place

his hands on her shoulders, but her arms were still crossed. "Maybe that's what I wanted to talk about, though. I'm not saying it has to be right this second, but... I don't want to be that woman in my thirties who struggles to get pregnant. I used to think working with the law would take up my youth, but since I can't officially practice in Belize yet I thought... you know... maybe a family?"

"A family? Like... like... like babies?" Kye asked, his face going pale.

"That's usually what a woman gets pregnant with, Kye."

"I... er... um..." He stepped back and scratched the back of his neck.

"Sir, I need to see you in the control room," Luca called from the open doorway.

"Thank God," Kye said under his breath. "We'll talk more about this soon," he said to Eliana. Giving her a quick kiss on the lips, he jogged off to join Luca, and they both disappeared down the cobblestone path. Eliana sighed in frustration and began packing up the meal they'd both barely touched.

"Not exactly how I wanted that conversation to go," she muttered and slammed the food back into her basket.

17

"See, here? This is what I was talking about right here," Luca said, pointing to the screen. Kye was leaning over the back of Luca's wheeled chair in the basement control room, staring at the screen. "I was looking at the tapes from last night, something small was triggering the sensors. I figured it was just an animal. Obviously, it wasn't anything big enough to set off the alarms, but then I saw this."

The computer room housed over twenty-five monitors that were all synced to their own camera, and five of them alternated angles for more sensitive spots like the front gate and the two side entrances for their beach property. The main desk in the room, Luca's command station, had all the bells and whistles anyone could need including a remote operation for the two drone guns at the main gate, and the master security alarm that would alert everyone on base as well as local authorities.

On the computer screen in front of them, Kye saw the heat generated an infrared image. Though it was off behind the tree line, it was clearly in the shape of a person. He could make out arms and legs, even though it was huddled at the base of a tree in a crouched position.

"Is this the only angle?" Kye asked, keeping his eyes firmly fixed on the image.

"Only one, sir," Luca confirmed. "I checked all the other cameras at the same timestamp, and there's nothing. Barely a bird flew by."

"Where is this one?"

"On the eastern side, just before the gates of the beach," Luca replied. He pulled out a map of the compound that had all the cameras and their radiuses in red. "Whoever he was must have come from the road here," Luca said, indicating the gray line that represented a street. "It's two miles of woods in every direction, but here, where the road bends, it's barely half a mile to the wall. That would be my guess."

"Do we have eyes up there? Can we tell what vehicle they're driving?" Kye asked, taking the map and looking it over.

"No, sir," Luca said, pinching the bridge of his nose. "We've done our best to keep the compound secure, but we can't have eyes everywhere. The more we run cameras, the more attention we draw to ourselves."

"Alright," Kye said, standing. "It's only one person. Let's hope it's a local who got a little too curious. For now, let's keep the floodlights off at night and have the night patrol equipped with night vision. Can you put in some overtime this week? I'd like you to oversee a couple of drone patrols. You can hook up the infrared camera to it, right?"

"Yeah, of course," Luca agreed, spinning around in his chair to watch Kye make for the door. "Is all this necessary for one little blip?"

"Probably not," Kye said grinning, "but I'd be the biggest jackass alive if I had all of this security and didn't use it."

Luca shrugged as he turned around in his chair and set to work equipping the drone helicopter.

"MAN, I need to talk to you," Kye said, bursting into the building. Grier was sitting at the end of the bar looking over his ledgers. The bar he had set up was a glorified food truck with a cantina-style roof, some tiki torches, and a few picnic tables. The walls were mostly old tin siding slabs he'd drilled into the concrete floor.

"Who's trying to kill us now?" Grier asked without looking up from the paperwork. Kye snuck around the backside of the bar and poured himself a glass of whiskey. "You gotta pay for that, man."

"Yeah, put it on my tab," Kye snapped and downed the glass with one long gulp. "I'm serious— I'm a dead man." Grier sighed and set aside his paperwork to look up at his friend. Though he'd sounded overdramatic, the panic on Kye's face was evident. He was scared shitless.

"Kye, settle down. It was one infrared blip. I'll spend a few days at the compound, and if we need we can call in a few troops from Texas. They can fly down, be here in a couple of days. No problem," Grier said and watched as Kye poured himself another glass.

"That's not what I'm talking about," Kye said, grimacing as the liquor burned his throat from how quickly he'd downed it.

"What is it then?" Grier asked, feeling Kye's nervousness was contagious.

"It's Eliana, she's talking about babies."

"Babies?" Grier asked, eyebrows knit together. "Like… human babies?"

"Yeah, human babies. Diapers. Bottles. You know…" He made a motion as though pushing something out of his crotch clearly pantomiming labor. "Babies."

"Why is she talking about babies? Who has a baby?"

"No one yet, thank God!" Kye said and filled his mouth with more of the strong alcohol.

"Then why is she talking about human babies?"

"Not just human babies, not just any babies, but like… our babies. Her babies with me," Kye said, jabbing a finger into his chest. Grier balked at him for a moment and reached over the counter for an empty glass and poured himself a drink from the bottle Kye was chugging away at.

"You're having a baby with Eliana? Let me process this," Grier said and drank. Kye swallowed his mouthful and shook his head.

"No, not yet, she's not pregnant. She said she wasn't, but I think she's disappointed about that. She was talking about going off her birth control and shit," Kye said in an almost whining voice.

"Did you act like this when she brought it up?"

"No, I kinda ran away…"

"So, what you're saying is she isn't pregnant, hasn't gone off the pill yet, but only mentioned it to you and you're freaking out?"

"Exactly," Kye said, and when his glass was empty, he refilled it. Grier sat back staring at his friend who was two shots shy of a nervous breakdown.

"Man, you're a pussy." The comment lingered in the air for a moment, then Kye glared at him."

"Man, fuck you!" Kye cursed and grabbed the bottle before sauntering toward the exit.

"No, seriously," Grier said, following his friend out. "You're being a total chump. So, she brought up kids; stop having a meltdown. She's a woman and at her age, she's probably already thinking about kids. Now that she's reunited with the love of her life, holed up in the most romantic paradise on earth, and lord knows you two are going at it like rabbits, it's only natural she's thinking about it. Honestly, you should have been thinking about it too."

"Grier, we've only been here six months. We haven't tracked down who was shooting at us in Monterrey, and who knows how safe we are. We haven't put the bunker to test…"

"Dude, shut up," Grier interrupted. "You're not scared of the compound being safe; you're just scared."

"I…" He was going to protest and say he wasn't scared, but he had to admit that he was. The moment he'd thought Eliana was telling him she was pregnant, the only image that flashed through his mind was staring at the brake lights of his dad's truck as it drove away leaving him on the side of the road with no family. "I can't be a dad, Grier. I don't know the first thing about being a dad."

"No guy does," Grier said casually. "You don't get to

some magical age and all of a sudden you know every-thing about parenting. It's a learning process. You make a mistake, you fix it and move on. That's just life."

"No, it's not just life; we're talking about a kid. A little baby."

"A human baby."

"Yes, a fucking human baby," Kye said, narrowing his eyes. "What if I make a mistake and permanently fuck this kid up?"

"Like abandon it and put it in the foster care system to grow up feeling unloved, unwanted, and alone?" Grier asked and took the bottle from Kye only to help him pour another, smaller, glass.

"Maybe not that drastic but…"

"That's what you're really scared of, though," Grier said knowingly. "You don't want what happened to you to happen to your kid, and you don't want to turn out like your old man. Or worse, Max."

"Grier," Kye said in a warning tone of voice. He thought about it for a moment as he stared inside his glass at the amber liquid. He'd been in a cold sweat all afternoon since she'd brought it up, and the idea that he would be responsible for raising a child made him more afraid than any gun he'd faced down. "Yeah, okay… you're right," he finally admitted.

"I know I am," Grier said casually and sipped his drink.

"What do I do about it?"

"Fuck if I know. I'm not Dr. Phil." Grier clinked the rim of his glass with Kye's and walked off, leaving his friend in that dangerous place between understanding but still not knowing a damn thing.

18

"We've got a bigger problem than some random person prowling around the gates," Kye said to the room of men. He'd pulled Matty, Luca, Douglas, Russell, and Grier into their weekly meeting two days early and handed each of them a map of the coast near their compound. They'd all been pulling double duty the last week since their prowler was spotted on infrared. Twice in the last seven days, the sensors had been triggered, but whoever it was had kept to the shadows just out of range of the cameras.

They were long past suspecting this was just a local who had wandered onto the property. True, they had a reputation with the locals of being a very wealthy establishment. There weren't many who lived in the area that possessed the kind of money Kye had stashed away for his retirement. Even Grier was living high off his pension he'd stashed away. But the compound also had a reputation for being welcoming and friendly, even charitable if not secretive. No one was allowed through the gate without an escort, but it wasn't uncommon especially for those looking to have their vehicles repaired.

Whoever was stalking the premises was likely doing recon. Always spotted near a different camera, a fast-moving shadow or a blip on the heat-seeking cameras, they were doing a damn good job of getting information on the outside. Not that it would help them. The moment the electric fence was engaged, they had only one option of getting inside and that was the front door. All electricity was run by internal generators, so there was no chance of having their power cut, and there were enough resources inside to feed them for months should they need to enter lockdown. Whoever was scouting them was likely a low-level bounty hunter looking for cash or notoriety. They'd be hard-pressed to find it here.

"It's been all over the news," Grier said, glancing over the weather map Kye had passed around. "They're calling it Hurricane Suzette. She's a real bitch."

"Putting it mildly, she's already wiped out three small islands between Jamaica and Cuba. Nearly obliterated the Cayman Islands, and is headed this way," Kye explained. "Now, she's losing steam and turning north.

I've been tracking it every ten minutes since dawn, but Suzette is moving quickly, and by the looks of it we're going to start getting some nasty weather before tonight is over."

"Can we evacuate?" Russell asked, setting his paper down. Having served in the Marines for eight years, he knew the damage a hurricane could do.

"We have a small skiff available for any of you that want to go. There's an evacuation taking place just south of us. The Red Cross will see you placed securely inland. You'll be fed, clothed, and housed until this is over. Grier and I have talked it over. We're going to hunker down here and ride it out. We think the worst of it will be over in the next forty-eight to seventy-two hours."

"Is that wise?" Matty asked. Clearly, his concern was for his family, and Kye gave him a small smile of understanding.

"We're not directly on the coast, and the reports show a tidal wave is unlikely. It's going to get rainy and windy really fast and hard. Like I said, any of you who want to go, you have our full resources behind you, and you know your job is waiting if you decide to return. If you decide to stay, we've got supplies and room in the main house for everyone. Grier and I are going to break our backs getting everything secured today. You all decide what you feel is best."

"Well, you know we're staying," Russell said, speaking for both he and his brother. "We'll get the power drills and start using the extra aluminum siding to secure the roof of the main house."

"Probably pull the gear in from the dock too," Douglas added. "The equipment should be safe if we can get the mechanic shop secured."

"Thanks, boys," Kye said fondly. They didn't wait for further instruction but left the room to get to it.

"You know I'm with you in spirit," Matty said, standing from his reclined position against the wall, "but I need to get my wife and kid out of here. You know Maggie is due in two months…"

"I was going to suggest it, but I wanted to leave the decision up to you," Kye interrupted, and the two men shook hands. "Take the Yukon and travel inland. Text me when you're somewhere safe," Kye instructed, and Matty clapped a hand on his shoulder in appreciation.

"I'll stay," Luca said shortly. "Don't want to put anyone out, but the town is going to need a lot of help once the storm clears. I want to be around to help with the cleanup."

"Come with me," Grier said, rising from the table. "Let's get the cameras pulled in, then we need to do a run into town. We'll need to make sure we've got enough fuel for the generators."

"Sounds good, boss," Luca said, and they each tossed Kye a wave as they left.

Kye stood there for a moment, hands on the table when he heard her feet shuffling above him. Looking up into the gallery, he saw Eliana watching from the banister. They exchanged small smiles before she turned to enter their bedroom. Things had been tense between them since their brief mentioning of babies in the days before. She'd been polite, but nothing more. And she was avoiding him.

Well, he'd be damned if she was going to blow hotter than the impending hurricane.

Kye was up the staircase in moments, and when he reached the bedroom, he saw her nailing boards over the windows on the balcony. Moving out the open door, he watched her fit the plank in place and hammer it into the siding.

"You're pretty good at that," he observed as he leaned against the railing behind her.

"Doesn't take a law degree to figure out how to use a hammer," she said flatly, and he grinned. Pushing himself off the railing, he held the next board in place for her as she held a nail in her mouth and began tapping the other one in place.

"Eli," he said softly. "I'm in love with you."

"I know you are," she said, not meeting his eyes, instead focusing intently on her nail.

"I want to marry you," he continued. She still didn't look up, but her hammer missed the mark on her next tap. "And I want to have kids with you." Now she looked up at him. Her brown eyes round and vulnerable.

"Don't say that unless you mean it…"

"Come here," he said, taking her hand and pulling her to her feet. He held her by the hips, and she rested her hands, one still containing the hammer, over his shoulders. "I'm not just saying that. I freaked out a little, I'll admit. I only just got you, after ten years of aching for you. The idea of having kids… as stupid as it sounds, I never put much thought into it. I had to earn you first."

"You didn't need to earn me…" she started, but he cut her off.

"I would never forgive myself if I hurt you in any way. Even more than that, if we had a child… if you had my child, and I let you down, wasn't a good father. I don't think I could bear it."

"You're afraid you're not going to be a good father?" she asked as though it was the most absurd question she'd ever heard. "You'd make an amazing father, Kye. I remember the way you looked after your younger siblings when you lived with the Duncans. You're the kindest, bravest, sweetest man I know."

"After everything I've been through, though…"

"That's what will make you a great dad," she interjected. "You've experienced the worst of it. You know what that pain is like. You'd never let something like that happen to anyone you loved." Kye could only nod. He didn't realize until that moment that he'd started to cry. A single tear rolled down his cheek, and Eliana brushed it away with her thumb. "There's no pressure to start a family right this moment, but I needed it to be a conversation."

"I want a family with you. I want you to be a mother and my wife and everything else. I want you to have everything," he said quickly, sincerely.

"I just want this," she said placing a hand over his heart. "I just want you."

"I'm yours. All yours."

KYE WAS RUNNING his hands down her bare arms as they lay in bed together. The rain was pelting the house outside, and the way the wind whipped through the air made a howling sound. "I can hear the sirens," Eliana murmured, her cheek pressed to his bare chest.

"We'll be okay," he said reassuringly. They'd dimmed the lights to conserve power, and the low lights granted a very romantic vibe, despite the raging weather around them. The compound was well placed on a small hill nearly a mile inland from the ocean so the risk of flooding was minimal. All the same, they had two sump pumps on standby ready to work.

All windows were boarded up, and the vehicles were safely stored in the stable turned garage. Kye felt secure knowing all the buildings were made of reinforced concrete and, at the worst, the dock would be destroyed. He'd been tracking the storm and if the Doppler was correct, they'd only get hit by the southern tip of it. Still, by the sounds of it, the weather was raging and though they couldn't see outside, the night was the blackest it had ever been.

"If this is how we're going to spend our time as the storm passes, I think more hurricanes should blow through," she teased as his hands found her ass under the covers. Giving her cheeks a firm squeeze, he hoisted her onto his lap and kissed her deeply. He was about to give her his hurricane when the walkie talkie on the nightstand screeched to life.

"Kye, we have a problem," Luca said from the other end. He was in the basement monitoring the storm from the computers.

"What is it?" Kye asked, holding the black device up to his mouth. "The storm?"

"Not exactly," Luca replied. Annoyed his attention was being pulled was from the naked woman straddling him, Kye snapped back.

"You know that prowler we've been keeping an eye on?"

"Yes?"

"Well, she's here."

"She?"

"Yeah. She. And she's at the front gate. She's saying something about Max."

19

"Grier, I want you on my left, Luca is operating the remote machine guns we left mounted on the gate. Douglas is on the patio with a rifle, and Russell is on the ground scouting for an ambush. Let's get out there, see what she wants, and get back inside. The storm isn't going to hold off forever."

"Let's go." Grier and Kye turned to see Eliana descending the stairs wearing jeans, a thick sweatshirt with a hood, and holding a gun in her right hand.

"What do you think you're doing?" Kye asked.

"You're not coming," Grier added.

"Like hell I'm not," Eliana protested. "Max is hunting all three of us. If this is some assassin or bounty hunter, I'm not hiding inside waiting to be killed."

"Suppose the moment we get to the gate, she puts a bullet between your eyes?" Kye asked angrily.

"Suppose she's perfectly harmless and desperately needs a place to get shelter from the storm? We can stand here making suppositions all day, but I'm going out there with you. I'm done being left behind, and I'm sure as hell not going to cower in a panic room while my home could potentially be getting attacked," she said in a very matter-of-fact tone.

"Eli…" Kye had started to warn, but she cut him off by chambering a round in her handgun.

"Let's go," she repeated and stepped toward the front door. Kye looked to Grier for assistance, but the taller man only shrugged and followed after Eliana. Clearly, this was an argument he wasn't going to win and didn't have time to fight anyway. Reluctantly, he trailed behind the two of them.

Grier opened the front door, and the black night slapped at them like a whip. The rain came down in long, pelting drops that flung themselves from the sky in a fury. The wind was a mixture of long gusts and short bursts that nearly knocked them over. The ground was slick and muddy, but they managed to stay on the path.

Kye took the lead when they reached the gate. Even over the storm, he could hear the woman at the gate shouting at the security camera. Dressed in all black, he couldn't make out a single distinguishing feature. Her anger was as potent as the hurricane. Her hands were clutching the steel bars, and she was yanking on the door trying to emphasize the point that she wanted to be let in.

"And I swear on my mother's grave if this door doesn't open in the next ten seconds, I'm going to blow the damn thing open!"

"I'd rather you didn't," Kye said, standing opposite her, but out of her arm's reach. "Who are you?"

"Who am I? I'm the person who's been screaming at your camera for damn near thirty minutes. I'm soaked through, and the wind is about to blow me away. Let me inside!" Her voice was shrill, but not in an obnoxious way. She was clearly a dominant personality and used to getting her way. The presumptuousness in her demeanor gave that away.

"Who are you?" Grier called again, his voice firm and unwavering. He and Eliana were standing eight paces back from Kye, guns drawn and aimed. She might have been imagining it, but Eliana felt Grier tense and straighten just a little more than usual.

"Open the door, you bloody bastard," the woman snapped and shook the bars. While not entirely accented, there was a hint of the United Kingdom in her voice, and it gave Eliana pause.

"Not until you tell us who you are and why you've come here," Kye retorted. "Before you argue, just remember that I have no problem leaving you out here to die." As if adding a deeper level to his threat, the wind picked up suddenly, and they all had to shield their eyes from the rain that stung like needles.

"I'm not here to kill you, if that's what you're wondering," she answered finally. "I've been scouting your base for the last week trying to find a way in…"

"We know, we saw you on infrared."

"Damn," she muttered, wiping a gloved hand down her masked face. It didn't escape anyone's notice that the black bandana over her mouth was similar to the ones the men in Jeeps wore when they were shot at in Monterrey. "I just need to speak to Grier. If I'm not mistaken, that's him standing just out of sight!" Kye and Eliana both turned to look at Grier who didn't lower his weapon in the slightest.

"Grier?" Eliana asked in a soft voice she hoped he could hear over the storm. He didn't change his posture, but glanced at her out of the corner of his eye.

"You say you're not here to kill us, but Max sent you?" Eliana asked, taking a few steps forward. "Is Max alive?"

"Listen," she said, clutching the bars tighter and pressing her face between two of them. "I will tell you everything. Please, just let me inside. I've been out in this storm for hours, and I can't feel my legs anymore." Her tone had gone soft, and her pleas made Eliana feel guilty. She looked at Kye with concern.

"Kye, let her in. We can talk to her inside…"

"No," he said firmly. When a crack of lightning struck overhead and the sound of tree limbs snapping in the wind echoed, he sighed and pulled the walkie talkie from his belt. "Open the door, Luca. Russ, Douglas, I want you at the main house."

A squawked reply came back over, and a second later the door began to move. The woman stepped back enough to avoid the door, and the moment it was open wide enough for her to enter, she slipped inside and stepped past Eliana and Kye.

"Come on, let's get inside and warmed up..." Eliana had started to say, but as soon as she turned to the woman, the black figure was launching herself over the edge of the path and tackling Grier. Eliana shrieked in surprise and raised her gun.

"Don't!" Kye said, knowing that in the dark with the two figures rolling around, she was just as likely to shoot Grier as the stranger. Kye and Eliana watched helplessly as the woman clawed and swung at Grier like a cornered cat. The fight was short though because in a quick thrust of his hips, Grier slammed the woman onto the ground and pinned her into the mud with one hand. His other hand held her wrist where she'd brandished a small knife no longer than her finger.

"Shoot her," Kye instructed, but Grier held up a hand to stop them.

"Don't shoot," he said in a tone that sounded uncharacteristically worried. "This pathetic little assassin isn't going to kill anyone." He took hold of her bandana and ripped it away from her face. Though caked with mud, her face was still pretty, and with her hood removed, they could see the wet tendrils of bright red hair sopping in the rain.

"Who is she?" Eliana asked in confusion.

"Fiona," she said through gritted teeth. Giving one last attempt to buck Grier off of her, she tried to twist her hips and counter his hold, but Grier was unyielding. Sighing in defeat, she glanced over at Kye and Eliana. "I'm Fiona Strong. Max's daughter."

* * *

"I THOUGHT you said Max didn't have any kids," Eliana whispered to Kye. They were all back inside now and had lit a fire in the fireplace. Though it sizzled with the rain that dripped through, it gave them enough warmth and light to continue their talk in the living room.

"Max said he didn't have any sons. I guess that was his way of avoiding the truth that he had a daughter," Kye shrugged.

"What if she's lying?" Eliana asked.

"I doubt it. Telling us she's the only child of our sworn enemy wouldn't gain her any friendships here. Plus," Kye added, "she's got Max's eyes. Same unmistakable metallic gray." They both looked over at Fiona who was leaning against the back of the couch. Grier was trying to hand her an icepack for her lip, and she snatched it away from him angrily.

"They know each other, I'm sure of it," Eliana said and sipped her mug of hot coffee she'd brewed.

"Let's find out how they know each other," Kye said and led her over to the duo. "Alright, Miss Strong…"

"Fiona."

"Fiona," Kye corrected, "we've got a few questions."

"I'm sure you do," she said almost sarcastically.

"First things first, you said Max sent you. Does that mean he's still alive?" Kye questioned. Fiona's eyes dropped, and she cleared her throat. "What was that?"

"Yes," she said a little louder, "but not exactly alive. He's on life support, last I knew anyway. The cancer beat him."

"When was the last time you heard from him?" Eliana asked.

"Directly?" she asked and glanced up at her. Eliana nodded. "Months ago. He was in the hospital with injuries to his face… to his eye. That's when he sent for me. I came to see him, and his last request was for me to track you down and kill you."

"That sounds like Max," Kye said flippantly. "So, you're here to kill us?"

"Fuck no!" she said, almost laughing. "If I was going to kill you I would have done it already."

"But you said that Max…"

"I haven't listened to a damn order my father has given to me since I was nine years old, and I'm not about to start now. No, I'm here for other reasons."

"Which would be?" Kye pressed.

"Personal," she said with a defiant look. Kye had been right about those eyes. The cold and calculating way she looked at them reminded Eliana very much of Max.

"You said Max sent for you? Were you living abroad?" Eliana asked, trying to defuse the tension. Kye was annoyed he wasn't getting answers, and Grier was standing half a step away from Fiona with hands balled into fists.

"Yeah, you could say that."

"Ireland," Grier added and broke his streak of silence. "Max sent her to Ireland. I was her security before she left the country."

"You make it sound so impersonal. We know each other a lot better than that," Fiona said in a suggestive manner. Eliana and Kye exchanged surprised looks.

"It's not like that," Grier said, cutting off their train of thought as though they'd spoken it out loud. "I was asked to keep her out of troubles… from time to time."

"That's not all!"

"Yes, it is!"

"Well, don't you blow hot and cold!" she said, clearly enjoying her ability to get under Grier's skin. Indeed, Eliana had never seen him so rattled. He looked torn between punching her and running from the room. If for no other reason than this, Eliana couldn't help but like the short red-haired woman.

"What is it that you want, exactly?" Grier asked, pinching the bridge of his nose.

"You and Kye Driscoll have gone and Max's two other commanders are dead, he's passed the mantle of MC president on to me," Fiona said in a powerful declaration, and three sets of eyebrows went up.

"What about Hamilton?" Kye asked.

"You think my dad can trust anyone after what you did?" She was shaking her head as though remembering something very painful. "So, the club is left to me. Seeing as the lot of you betrayed my father and the Screaming Demons, I'm here to collect the debt you owe."

"I thought you weren't going to kill us!" Eliana said, very confusedly.

"Oh, I'm not," Fiona said quickly. "I just want Grier to take me to bed."

All four of them fell silent as her statement blew through them harder than the hurricane level winds outside, then three of them all looked at Fiona and cried a booming, "What!"

"You came all this way to have sex with Grier?"

"I'm not taking you to bed!"

"I'm so confused."

They were all talking over one another but were silenced when Fiona started laughing loudly. "I'm not looking to fuck him because he's just so damn cute," she cooed and pinched Grier's cheek. He quickly swatted her hand away. "My claim on the club is weak because I'm a woman. To hell with modern feminism, an MC club is the embodiment of a patriarchal dictatorship. What I need to solidify my stake is a son. Grier is going to give me one." The way she said it, so precisely and easily, you'd think she was reciting some written rule in a handbook.

"I… I don't know what to say to that," Eliana stammered as she looked between Kye and Grier. "Is that an actual thing clubs do?"

"No!" Grier snapped, but Kye looked less convinced.

"Actually," he said, running his fingers through his wet hair, "if a new MC President is owed a debt inherited by the former president, especially a blood bond, the new president has the discretion to call in the debt under any circumstance."

"A life for a life, I think it's fair," Fiona reasoned. "You killed Max, I get a baby."

"You said Max isn't dead," Grier argued.

"Not yet, but soon, very…" she explained.

"Then we didn't kill Max at all," Grier snapped.

"He is as good as dead since Kye stabbed him!"

"You said it was cancer!"

"Which only made him weaker because he got stabbed in the bloody eye! Aren't you lot supposed to be clever?"

"I'm not fucking you!"

"Yes, you are, pretty boy, now drop trou and get it up!"

"You're a fucking lunatic!"

"Just imagine how batshit crazy I'll be with pregnancy hormones!"

As the two exchanged heated jabs, Kye and Eliana slowly backed out of the room. Clearly, this discussion needed to be left between the two of them. Besides that, they were both still dripping wet in their soaked clothes, and as Fiona was now unarmed and being dealt with by Grier, they were ready to excuse themselves to bed.

Kye called over the walkie for the others to stand down as he and Eliana slid into their bedroom. They could still hear Fiona and Grier shouting at each other, and they couldn't help but laugh.

"She's going to murder him if he doesn't sleep with her," Eliana said as she helped Kye out of his wet clothing.

"He'll sleep with her," Kye replied confidently.

"He will?"

"Oh yeah," Kye said and when he was standing naked, he began assisting Eliana in removing her wet clothes. "If he doesn't do it to clear our debt, he'll do it because he's insanely attracted to her."

"You think he likes her?"

"Likes her?" Kye asked incredulously. "No, he can't stand her. Doesn't mean he doesn't want to bend her over the couch and…"

"I get the picture," Eliana said, holding a hand up to stop him. They were both naked now and shivering from the cold. Ducking under the covers, they wrapped their arms around each other and their lips connected. "I hope the storm doesn't wipe out the clinic. I need to pick up my prescription," she said while he was kissing her neck. "You know, my little pink pills?"

Kye propped himself up on his forearms as he hovered over her. "What if…" he began, and his blue eyes found her brown ones. "What if you didn't pick up your prescription?"

"You mean… go off my birth control?"

"Yeah."

"But eventually you know that I'd get…"

"Pregnant?" he asked. "Yeah. I know you would. I think that's the idea."

"You mean it?" she asked, eyes brimming with tears. Kye only nodded, a soft smile tugging at his lips. She pulled him down into a hard kiss, and when his erection found her heat, he pressed into her with no hesitation.

The storm raged outside and struggled to match the intense argument from the living room, but neither held a candle to the passionate tempest between Eliana and Kye.

20

When the storm finally subsided, an eerie calm overtook the compound. Eliana was the first to wake the next morning, and when she stepped outside, the sky was such a brilliant blue it was hard to imagine only hours before there was utter chaos. Palm fronds and boards littered the ground, and the sopping wet earth squished underfoot.

"Be careful," Grier said, stepping outside. Needing to busy herself, Eliana was already gathering up the debris and making a pile in the courtyard they could burn down. "We're mostly safe, but I see some scattered glass shards."

"I can grab some of the work gloves from the shop," Eliana offered. She saw the hesitant look on Grier's face, and it gave her pause. "Where's our little friend?" she asked without taking a single step closer to the old stables.

"Asleep in my room." Eliana's eyebrows rose. "I didn't have sex with her!" he said quickly.

"I didn't say you did."

"You were thinking it," Grier grumbled, and Eliana laughed. "What?"

"I've never seen you like this. You're usually cool as a cucumber and now you're all bristly like a porcupine," Eliana said and grabbed the other end of the log Grier was dragging off the path. Together they carried it to the makeshift bonfire pile.

"I'm not a porcupine, and I'm not bristly; I just didn't sleep well," he defended, and Eliana rolled her eyes. "Well, how would you feel if the freedom of your friend's lives depended on you sleeping with someone you'd only seen as a younger sibling?"

"I don't think it's as dramatic as all that," Eliana stated and brushed her hands free of dirt. "Fiona doesn't really expect you to impregnate her."

"She sure as hell does!" Grier snapped. "You heard her! If there's one thing I know about Fiona Strong is that the second she gets a thought into her head, there's no beating it out of her."

"If you don't want to have sex with her then don't; she can't force you. That would be rape, and she doesn't seem like a rapist."

"She might!" Grier said with his hands on his hips. "She's been after me for years, and now she's got me by the proverbial balls. If I don't give her what she wants, then she's going to call in the debt you and Kye owe. Now that she knows where you're living, you'll have MC bounty hunters so far up your asses you'll be spitting handlebars." Eliana laughed, and Grier grew more agitated. "I fail to see the humor in this."

"Grier, you're scared of her!"

"I am not!"

"Yes, you are, look at you! You're flustered and paranoid. Who knew all it took to rattle the great, stoic Grier Owen was a five-foot-five redhead." Eliana couldn't keep the amusement from her voice if she tried. "I promise, if it comes down to it, I'll defend your virtue!"

"You're a real pain in the ass, you know that?" he asked and tossed two more handfuls of fronds onto the stack.

"I do," she agreed and stopped to watch him as he took out his anger on an overturned barrel. "How do you know Fiona anyway? From what Kye said, no one knew Max had any kids."

"That's the way he wanted it. For some reason, Max thought I was the dumb one, but it's not hard to figure things out when I was asked to watch this pain in the ass teen that wouldn't stop getting me into more trouble than I would have liked. Some of the seniors at the club know about her, but they never talked about her in the club. I guess Max wanted it that way."

"It's clear she's got it out for you. She must have had a crush on you all these years," Eliana pieced together.

"Yeah, and now she's exploiting that!" Grier was back to sounding pissed.

"What are you going to do? And let me just add before you answer that, Kye and I do not expect you to sleep with her or attempt to get her pregnant. If it comes down to it, we're prepared to pay our debts ourselves. We wouldn't have all that we do if you hadn't been around, Grier. We owe you everything," Eliana said sincerely.

"Well, I don't want to fuck her, I can tell you that much," Grier said and kicked a rock with the toe of his shoe. "I did agree to go back with her, though. To the states…"

"You did?" Eliana asked surprised.

"Kye paid the blood price to be relieved from the Demons, I didn't. I'm still a full patch member, and I don't want to be on the run from them. Whether I stay a Demon or not, I'm not going to live on the outside or under the radar. Fiona is going to face a lot of opposition taking on the mantle of president. I'm hoping if I head back with her and help her ascend, that she'll see she doesn't need a son to have authority."

"She's still going to want to sleep with you," Eliana said teasingly, and Grier glared at her. "After you help her, will you come back?"

"I don't know… I don't think so," he admitted. Eliana felt a twinge of pain well up inside her. "This is yours and Kye's story, not mine. He'll always be my brother, and as much as I can't stand you most of the time, I see how happy you make him. I've done my bit getting you here; it's time for me to move on."

"Grier," Eliana said, biting her lip. She walked straight up to him and wrapped him in a tight hug. "I can't stand you either," she said, sniffling. His shoulders shook with a small laugh, and he hoisted her into a tight embrace. "You'll always have a place here with us."

"Yeah, well," Grier said, trying to cover a sniffle with a cough, "I'll probably still be able to hear you two having sex all the way in Maine." They both laughed, and that was when they saw Kye standing in the doorway to the house. He'd clearly been listening to their conversation. His eyes looked melancholy, and his arms were crossed.

"When do you leave?" he asked somberly. Grier stuffed his dirty hands into his pockets and shrugged.

"Knowing Fiona, soon," he admitted. "I was going to head into town and see what condition the airport is in."

"Airport is fine," Kye said, walking the few steps from the house to join them on the pathway. "Had the news on earlier. The airport and major hospitals are all fine. The nearby village is almost decimated, though. A lot of people lost their homes."

"I need to check on Hela," Eliana said, kicking herself for not remembering her friend. "Grier, I'll go into town with you!"

"I think we should all go," Kye suggested. "Luca said the compound was spared any major damage. The dock was destroyed, but we knew that was going to happen. Douglas and Russel are already gathering timber to repair. I think the best thing we can do is go into town and start helping them repair."

"Really?" Eliana asked, feeling an overwhelming sense of pride. Kye wrapped his arm around her shoulders.

"What's the point of having all of this and money if we're not putting it to good use? I spent a lot of time gaining profit off drugs and guns and, even without knowing it, prostitution and trafficking. I think it's time I did some good to balance the scales," Kye said reasonably. Eliana stood on her toes and kissed him.

"A lot of people will need your help, man," Grier said, clapping his shoulder. "You're a good man. Don't spend your life feeling guilty about things you can't go back and change."

"There's the wise sage," Eliana teased and wrapped an arm around Grier's waist as the three of them walked inside. "We're going to miss all your prudent advice when you're gone."

"I'll buy you a box of fortune cookies," he goaded, and Eliana laughed.

"Hey!" All three of them turned to look at the woman walking down the stairs. Having cast aside her baggy black clothes from the night before, Fiona had raided Eliana's closet and was dressed in a purple tube top and very short shorts.

Her previous attire lent nothing to her figure, but there was no mistaking the robust curves of the woman moving toward them. Her chest was bursting from the fabric and sans bra, her nipples were taut and standing at full attention. Her waist was petite, and her hips were round and full. Thin legs with shapely thighs, her curly red hair was flowing wildly around her shoulders. Both Kye and Grier stood with mouths gaping. Eliana furrowed her brow and pushed Kye's mouth shut with a single finger.

"Uh, er, good morning," he greeted, trying to recover himself.

"Good morning," Fiona said in a friendly voice to Eliana and Kye. Turning her sharp gaze to Grier, she placed her hands on her thin waist. "You!" she said, jabbing him in the chest with a finger. "You ready to give me a baby?"

21

"Alright, don't get sentimental on me," Grier said with a grin as he hugged Eliana. Her brown eyes were red with tears, and black mascara streaks stained her face. She hugged him tightly, and he kissed her on the top of the head. They were standing on the runway of the private airstrip, behind them their old friend Alberto had the engine to his plane running. Soon Grier and Fiona would be off, back to Mexico City and then home to the United States.

"I'm not sad you're leaving. I'm happy you're finally leaving," Eliana said belligerently. Grier smiled broader.

"Sure, you are," he said and brushed a tear off her cheek with his thumb. "Come here, you bastard," Grier said, pulling Kye into a tight hug. They clapped each other on the back and both forced a chuckle.

"You'll come back and visit," Kye said decidedly. "We want you here when the baby is born."

"Kye, we don't even know if I'm pregnant yet," Eliana said, slapping his shoulder. Though they'd been trying to conceive since the night of the hurricane almost a month ago now, she had only started showing small signs, like a missed cycle, in the last week.

"Promise?" Kye asked, ignoring Eliana and keeping his eyes on Grier.

"Wouldn't miss it, man. I'll be here for whatever you need," he said sincerely, and the two shook hands. Their feeling of brotherly love palpable.

"You know who isn't having a baby?" Fiona called as she pushed herself off the railing to the staircase that led up to the plane. "Me! What are we going to do about that?" she asked, elbowing Grier in the ribs.

"Play nice, you two; it's a long flight," Kye said and shook Fiona's hand. "Thanks for clearing our debt, by the way. It feels good to breathe easy for a change."

"Yes, thank you!" Eliana added.

"No problem. I'm the first person to say my dad is a colossal jackass, God bless him," she said, smiling. To her surprise, Eliana hugged her as the plane engine revved, signaling it was time to go. "Well, good luck, you two! I'm sure you'll do well in your little slice of heaven here. Lord knows you've done quite the job restoring the little village,"

Fiona said fondly. She'd never admit it out loud, but she liked Eliana and Kye. They loved each other, and she was begrudgingly jealous of the way Kye looked at Eliana. Fiona hoped to one day have that kind of love. "Let's go, jerk!" she said and slammed her bag into Grier's arms.

"If the plane crashes, don't send out a search team. Just let me burn to death in peace," Grier said to Kye and Eliana as he turned and made his way to the steps. Kye and Eliana wrapped their arms around each other for comfort as they watched their friend depart. Whether he liked it or not, Grier was going to be genuinely and sincerely missed.

As a matter of reluctant feelings, Grier couldn't help staring at Fiona's ass in those tight jean shorts as she climbed the steps in front of him. Despite the not so gangly babysitting, he remembered the woman in front of him now was all lips, hips, and tits, and he'd be crazy not to notice. She seemed perfectly content to flaunt her assets at him whenever she got the chance. He learned quickly to stay away from her.

"Be a good boy, and I'll indoctrinate you into the mile-high club," she teased, throwing him a sexy wink. Grier swallowed hard but managed an eye roll. "Sit by me," she said, yanking on his hand and pulling him into the seat next to her.

"We have the entire plane, why do I have to sit by

you? There are literally ten other seats I can sit in," Grier complained but made no move to stand.

"Because I've forgotten my pillow, and I need your fat arm," she said flatly. Hooking her arm with his, she leaned her head on his bicep.

"My arm isn't fat," he grumbled, and Fiona pinched him. "Ow!"

"Pillows don't talk!"

"I'm not a pillow!" he protested and tried to pull his arm away.

"Bitch, I'm your club president. If I say you're a pillow then you're a goddamn pillow!" Fiona snapped and grabbed his arm back, resuming her earlier position.

"You're never going to let me…"

"Did I forget to mention, you're a silent pillow?" Grier gritted his teeth but decided she wasn't going to relent on this argument. He sighed and allowed her to rest her head on his arm for the duration of the flight.

They'd only been in the air twenty minutes when he noticed she'd fallen asleep. Her breathing was even, and she snored softly. He even noticed a tiny line of drool from her mouth, and he tried not to laugh. She made a moaning noise as she shifted and pulled him closer. The sound sent a jolt through him and despite his hesitations about her, his body clearly liked the sound of her moaning because the front of his jeans became a bit tighter.

With her head now on his shoulder, he had a face full of her strawberry scented hair, and he rested his cheek on the soft curls. He had to admit, she was enjoyable when she was silent. Grinning and closing his eyes to welcome a restful flight himself, he silently admitted… he enjoyed her when she was awake and feisty too.

DARK DESIRES
~ A billionaire dark romance series ~
Dark Desire
Dark Rules
Dark Secret
Dark Time
Dark Truth

BARRE TO BAR
~ A billionaire second chance series ~
Dancing With Lies
Dancing With Temptation
Dancing With Doubt
Dancing With Guilt
Dancing With Redemption

TWISTED INTENTION
~ A billionaire revenge romance series ~
Twisted Beauty
Twisted Love
Twisted Fate

Mafia's Obsession
~ A hot mafia romance series ~
Mafia's Dirty Secret
Mafia's Fake Bride
Mafia's Final Play

Screaming Demons
~ An MC romance series full of suspense ~
Rough Start
Rough Ride
Rough Choice
Rough Patch
Rough Return
Rough Road
Rough Trip
Rough Night
Rough Love

Standalone Contemporary Romance
Billionaire in Vegas
Billionaire Hunt

Billionaire's Game

Billionaire Retreat

Billionaire On Air

A Chance To Love

Somebody To Love

Not Mine To Love

Check out Summer's entire collection at

www.summercooper.com/books

ABOUT SUMMER COOPER

Thank you so much for reading. Without you, it wouldn't be possible for me to be a full-time author. I hope you enjoy reading my books as much as I do writing them.

Besides (obviously!) reading and writing, I also love cuddling my dogs, shouting at Alexa, being upside down (aka Yoga) and driving my family cray-cray!

Get in touch at
hello@summercooper.com
www.summercooper.com

facebook.com/summercooperauthor
instagram.com/summercooperauthor
goodreads.com/summercooper
bookbub.com/profile/summer-cooper

www.ingramcontent.com/pod-product-compliance
Lightning Source LLC
Chambersburg PA
CBHW031230210726
48287CB00003B/724